"I'm

Jo nodded silently and willed the emotional tears not to fall. "I'm sorry I didn't tell you, Declan. I wanted to, but it's not the sort of thing you can add as a postscript to a letter, is it?"

But her first instinct had been to call him. All she'd wanted was his arms around her, telling her it would be all right. Declan was *always* the person she ran to when she was in trouble.

"I won't let you shut me out, Jo."

"Whatever made you think I'd try? But we didn't plan this. You didn't want to become a father, at least not to *my* child. We can't pretend we're suddenly in love...."

She's sexy,
successful...
and
PREGNANT!

Relax and enjoy our new series of stories about spirited women and gorgeous men, whose passion results in pregnancies...sometimes unexpected! Of course, the birth of a baby is always a joyful event, and we can guarantee that our characters will become besotted moms and dads—but what happened in those nine months before?

Share the surprises, emotions, dramas and suspense as our parents-to-be come to terms with the prospect of bringing a new little life into the world.... All will discover that the business of making babies brings with it the most special love of all....

Look out next month for:
The Unexpected Baby (#2040)
by Diana Hamilton

KIM LAWRENCE

Accidental Baby

TORONTO • NEW YORK • LONDON
AMSTERDAM • PARIS • SYDNEY • HAMBURG
STOCKHOLM • ATHENS • TOKYO • MILAN • MADRID
PRAGUE • WARSAW • BUDAPEST • AUCKLAND

ISBN 0-373-12034-6

ACCIDENTAL BABY

First North American Publication 1999.

CHAPTER ONE

LIAM RAFFERTY stared down at the sleeping figure beside him with a stunned expression. In a distracted manner he ran his fingers through his tousled dark hair. In profile her nose was tip-tilted and covered with a light sprinkling of freckles. Her long, dark eyelashes were tipped with gold and when her eyes opened he knew they would be deep green flecked with bronze.

When she woke... His fist went to his mouth and he bit back a groan. Abruptly the sleeping figure began to move, unfurling from the foetal position and rolling onto her back—arms above her head with her fingers pushed into the shoulder-length Titian-red tangle of curls that covered her small head. The sinuous undulations of her slim body caused the cotton sheet to slide down.

Liam, who had been about to do something sensible and decisive—like get some clothes on—paused. Not even the harshest critic could have found anything to criticise about her breasts, and Liam was by no means harsh. Her skin was milky pale and the light sprinkling of freckles over the uppermost curves was kind of cute. In the dark they'd just about fitted into the palm of—whoa, boy! He firmly shut off access to that particular memory.

Don't panic, just think sensibly, calmly, he told himself firmly. Problem was the visual feast on offer was incredibly distracting. Would she wake if I just sort of pulled up the...? Too late! At least his eyes had been on her *face* when her sleepy eyes opened. If she'd caught him ogling!

A dreamy smile curved Jo Smith's generous lips. 'Hi,

Liam,' she murmured sleepily. She froze mid-stretch and her eyes opened to their fullest extent. 'Liam?' Her eyes ran down his bronzed torso and a strangled squeak escaped her lips. A firm, 'We didn't?' was swiftly followed by a wail of, 'We did!'

This was one of those situations, he reflected, when your imagination couldn't prepare you for just *how* bad a situation was going to be. Despite his best intentions, Liam's self-control slipped for just a second. It had been doing that a lot recently! Jo's eyes followed the direction of his gaze and she snatched up the sheet and pulled it up to her chin, giving him the sort of look that made him feel like a defiler of purity.

'Try and keep this in proportion, Jo. It's not *that* bad.'

'Not that bad!' She went pink. Was he mad? This was worse than bad—this was a disaster.

'I don't blame you for hating me. I deserve it...' he began miserably.

'Don't be stupid, I don't hate you,' she returned impatiently.

God, men could be so obtuse sometimes—even Liam. Couldn't he see this changed everything? Things could never be the same again. They'd thrown away something precious and rare for a moment's... The clarity of her thoughts lost a certain something as she honestly acknowledged it had taken more than a moment the first time, and as for the second! A tide of heat washed over her skin leaving it pink and tingling.

'You don't?' That was something. He gave a sigh of relief, but the wariness in his blue eyes remained. 'I wouldn't blame you if you did,' he continued, quite determined to shoulder full responsibility. 'I took advantage of you when you were at your most vulnerable.'

'The way I recall it I didn't exactly fight you off with a stick,' she responded drily.

Liam cleared his throat and his gaze slid away from hers. I knew it! she thought. He can't even look at me. God, what have we done? One crazy, stupid slip and a lifetime's friendship goes down the toilet.

'That's not the point,' he said stiffly. 'I'm to blame.'

'Have you any idea how ridiculous you sound, Liam Rafferty, talking like a character in a Victorian melodrama when you're stark, staring naked?' Even in her present state of agitation she couldn't help giving an appreciative little sigh at how amazingly good his body actually was— her appreciation was purely aesthetic, of course. She wriggled into sitting position, bringing the thin cotton sheet around her like a tent.

'For pity's sake, Jo, I'm trying to say I'm sorry!' he said, regarding her with growing irritation.

'Charming!' she replied, choosing to take exception to this apology.

'Meaning?'

'Meaning it was that awful, was it?' Her lower lip quivered ever so slightly. 'Was it?' She silently cursed the note of anxiety that had crept into her voice.

'You know it wasn't, Jo.' This time it was Jo who couldn't maintain eye contact.

'Right, good, excellent...' Briefly she closed her eyes in silent despair. What *do* I sound like?

The wooden bed-head creaked as Liam's broad shoulders came to rest against it. 'You're not crying, are you, Jo?'

'Of course I'm not crying!' she returned, insulted that he could think she was that weak and *wet*. She'd always confidently denied the assertions of friends who said a man and woman couldn't have a totally platonic relationship.

Liam was her best friend; it was almost coincidental that he was a man. Circumstances had conspired to draw them together almost from birth: the proximity of their homes in rural East Anglia; the fact that their mothers had been school friends, and, whilst her father was the local vet, his was a successful horse-breeder. Leaving home and pursuing diverse careers hadn't weakened the bond between them.

She felt his arm slide across the wooden frame just above her shoulders and then quite suddenly he withdrew it. That made her want to cry quite badly. Their friendship had always been a tactile one—that he had to *think* about touching her now and then decide not to was a sad reflection of the new shape of things...

'It started with a hug,' he reminded her gruffly.

He could still read her mind, then; some things didn't change.

'That *bastard* hurt you so much I wanted to make you feel better. Then what do I do?' He hit his clenched fist into his open palm and the slapping sound made Jo jump.

He *had* made her feel better—very much better! 'You were the one that tried to stop.' She could feel her cheeks burning with mortification at the memory. 'I wouldn't let you. Don't go all hair-shirty on me, Liam.' I wonder if there are any buttons left on his shirt? She gulped as she recalled how she'd torn the garment off him.

'A man doesn't take advantage of a woman like that,' he maintained stubbornly.

'You're a rat, heel, skunk. There—satisfied? Does it make you feel any better?' she demanded tartly. 'Are you going to let your urge to be noble ruin our friendship? It's not as if we're going to make a habit of this, is it?' she pointed out practically.

I'm speaking rhetorically, she told herself. All the same,

when his laughter came it was much too spontaneous for her taste. He could have at least pretended to think about it, she thought indignantly.

'You're right, Jo.' This time his arm did go around her shoulders but Jo didn't relax into his embrace. 'We should just forget this ever happened.' He couldn't disguise the relief in his voice.

If the circumstances had been different Jo had no doubt that would have been exactly what she would have done. However, fate had stepped in to make that an impossibility for her.

'Did you have a nice walk, dear?'

'Lovely, thanks, Dad.' The wind along the beach had made her cheeks glow. 'I went farther than I meant to.' She released the Velcro fastening on her waterproof jacket and shook back her hair. 'What time are they expecting us?'

'Half eight, but if you're feeling too tired?'

'Don't fuss, Dad, there's an angel,' she pleaded. Her pleasure at all the pampering had already turned to impatience.

'You're meant to be taking things easy this weekend,' he protested with a worried frown.

'I am. If I relax much more I'll disintegrate.' Laughing, she went upstairs, mentally planning what she had in her wardrobe that would be suitable for the informal meal. She really would have to do some serious shopping very soon.

She'd thought her loose apple-green silky shirt was perfect, hiding a multitude of sins. Then she saw her sixteen-year-old sister in a minuscule miniskirt and skinny-rib top that left her tanned midriff bare. Her legs in knee-length leather platform boots went on for ever. Jo immediately felt extremely old and the size of a house.

'Won't you be cold, Jessie?' Bill Smith asked casually as he averted his eyes from his daughter's eye catching ensemble with a pained expression.

Jessie exchanged a grin with her elder sister. 'He's so subtle,' she said admiringly. 'What do you think, Jo?' She gave a twirl.

'You look great, Jessie,' she replied honestly.

'Yeah, I know.' she said, preening herself in front of the mirror with a smug expression. 'You're looking a bit podgy, Jo, if you don't mind me saying so.'

'Thanks a lot.' Jo received this news with admirable equanimity.

'Jessie!' Bill Smith protested.

'I'm kidding, Dad, just kidding,' Jessie replied, her shoulders shaking with laughter.

'Let me look at you.'

'Yes, Aunty Maggie,' Jo said meekly as the older woman placed her hands on her shoulders and examined her face with keen eyes. 'Will I pass?'

'You may smile, but your mother, God rest her, would have expected me to keep an eye on you. Wouldn't she, Pat?'

'Indeed she would, but don't keep them standing out there in the hall, woman. Come along in.'

The fire in the grate of the high-ceilinged Victorian drawing room was as warm as the welcome. Aunt Maggie had been her mother's best friend and this house had been a second home to Jo during her childhood.

'Jo!' Jessie, who stepped into the room in front of her, yelled. 'Why didn't you tell us Liam would be here?'

'I didn't know,' Jo said faintly as she was carried over the threshold by a combination of her Uncle Patrick's strong, guiding arm and an avalanche of goodwill.

'She didn't say a word, Liam,' Jessie was saying as she hung around the neck of the glamorous son of their next-door neighbours. 'We all thought you were digging up sleaze and exposing baddies behind the Iron Curtain.' She ruffled his collar-length wavy dark hair and grinned affectionately into his blue eyes. She'd decided recently that older men were fascinating and Liam must be almost *thirty* now.

'The Iron Curtain dissolved some time back.' He placed her firmly back down on her feet. 'Don't they teach you anything in school these days?'

In a daze Jo watched her father move forward to shake the hand of the tall, rangy figure who stood with his back to her. 'Pat tells me you've been digging into the archives in Moscow. Something interesting on the burner?'

'Could be,' Liam replied easily, 'but it's early days.'

'I read that article you did on the working conditions in sugar plantations on the Dominican Republic. It was an outstanding piece,' Bill Smith said warmly.

'The photographer I was working with was the best.'

'He's so modest,' Maggie Rafferty said fondly. She was justifiably proud of her son's reputation as a top investigative journalist. 'He's working on another book, you know.'

'Modest!' Pat at her elbow mocked gently. Jo wasn't fooled; she knew he was every bit as proud of their son as his wife. Liam's last book had stayed in the best-seller list for three months, which was pretty good for a critically acclaimed *serious* tome.

Liam turned around at the sound of his father's mocking laughter and saw Jo for the first time. His smile didn't fade, but it did freeze as though his facial muscles were momentarily paralysed. She could see the falseness, but she rather envied him his composure. *He'd* been expecting to see her, she reminded herself. It was all so ridiculously normal she wanted to laugh. Bad time for hysterical outbursts, Jo.

It was the very first time since that eventful morning-after that she'd actually seen him in the flesh, so to speak. There had been nothing deliberate about this; his job meant his lifestyle was gypsy-like. It had always been usual for them not to see each other for several months at a stretch. They'd written and spoken on the phone just as if it had never happened. But then that was the way they'd decided to play it, wasn't it? And from Liam's point of view it was probably working.

If Liam had felt any awkwardness at seeing her, he certainly recovered fast. He moved forward and kissed her on each cheek before pushing her to arm's length, very much as his mother just had, and warmly examining her face.

'I do believe you're putting on weight, Jo, around the face,' he said, a slight frown creasing his brow. 'It suits you,' he concluded with a smile. In the past he'd teased her about her fragile frame.

'Of course she's putting on weight, silly boy,' his mother put in in an indulgent tone.

'*I* got told off for telling her she's fat,' Jessie observed indignantly, sinking down into an armchair and helping herself to a handful of nibbles.

'She isn't fat,' their father put in.

'Yet!' Jessie chortled.

'Mary was the size of a house with Jessie early on, but she kept her figure until quite late on with you. You'll probably be the same with the first,' Bill recalled, frowning at his younger daughter as she stuffed another handful of bite-size delicacies into her mouth. 'You'll spoil your meal.'

They all assumed! Of course they all assumed he

knew—why wouldn't they? If Jo had been planning how to share this news with Liam, which she hadn't, this particular route wouldn't have been favourite! It was something she had been going to get around to eventually, of course, but not just yet. She had been a bit hazy about when the *right* time might be. One thing she knew for certain: it wasn't now! Liam had taken an involuntary step away from her and his gaze inevitably dropped to her waist, which was still almost as trim as it had been.

'Good God,' he said in a strangled voice, 'you're pregnant!'

'He doesn't know,' Jessie's youthful voice piped up. 'I thought you two told each other everything.'

'Not everything, it would seem,' Liam said grimly.

'Well, now you know,' Jo said casually. He wouldn't necessarily assume...

She saw immediately that this faint hope had been misplaced. Also, her casual tone hadn't gone down well at all; the white line around his compressed lips was a dead giveaway.

'Last but not least.' His voice sounded strangely unfamiliar to Jo.

'Can I get you a drink, Bill? I know you're off duty, but I was hoping you'd look in on the foal before dinner,' Pat Rafferty asked, blissfully ignorant of the storm clouds gathering. 'Girls, what can I get you?'

'Gin and tonic,' said the imperturbable Jessie.

'Give her a Coke, Pat,' Bill interjected.

'Worth a try.' Jessie was philosophical.

'How *could* you, Jo?' Liam's raw, throbbing words ripped through the normality of casual chatter.

Suddenly the whole room was looking from her to Liam with startled incomprehension. 'I don't want to talk about it now.' *Please* no scene.

He cruelly ignored the silent plea in her eyes. Why hadn't she ever noticed how hard and yes—*cruel* his expression could be? There was something bordering on the austere in the hard-angled planes and contours of his face. She began to shiver and couldn't stop—being intimidated by Liam of all people seemed a little crazy.

'Come on, now, lad, I can see it's a bit of a shock, but it's not really any of our concern, is it?' Pat said, placing a restraining hand on his son's arm.

Liam's eyes only left her face long enough to flicker briefly in his father's direction. 'I'd say my child is my concern, wouldn't you?'

The instant's silence was deafening and then suddenly everyone began talking at once.

'I'm going to be a grandmother again,' Maggie said faintly, sinking into a chair.

Jessie's eyes were sparkling with interest. 'I knew they shared *everything* but I didn't know they shared *that* too!' she whooped. 'It gives a whole new meaning to "joined at the hip".'

'Jessica! That's enough,' her father barked.

'Is this true, Liam?' Pat asked slowly, shaking his head in disbelief.

'Ask Jo,' Liam replied, his ice-blue eyes daring her to contradict him.

'I'll never forgive you for this as long as I live!' she declared passionately.

'That might not be very long,' he shot back equally grimly.

Maggie surged to her feet and clapped her hands together. 'I'm so happy,' she declared, tears pouring unchecked down her cheeks. 'I always knew you two were meant for each other.' She enfolded Jo in a warm embrace. 'You two, at last. A grandmother, I can't believe it.'

'I'm having some difficulty adapting to it myself, Mother.' He shot Jo a baleful look over Maggie's shoulder.

Maggie released Jo only to clasp her son to her maternal bosom. 'When are you getting married?' she sniffed.

'Married?' Riding on the crest of his righteous anger, this question brought Liam down to earth with a bang, and Jo could hear the crash. The hypocritical pig, she fumed.

'Yes, Liam,' she asked innocently, 'when *are* you going to make an honest woman of me?'

'A wedding!' Jessie squeaked, forgetting for a moment her teenage cool and general lack of interest. 'Can I be bridesmaid?'

'I think Jo and I need to discuss these things in private.'

'Oh, yes, you're very big on private now, aren't you? Pity you didn't think of that earlier. We don't need to discuss anything, Liam Rafferty, because I wouldn't marry you if you were the last man on earth!' she concluded with enough passion to compensate for lack of originality. 'This is *my* baby. I'm sorry, Aunt Maggie,' she said as the older woman burst into tears again. 'Now look what you've done!' she shouted, turning on Liam. 'It's all your fault!'

'Don't think I'm not aware of that fact.'

Jo's head came up with a snap. 'I knew it!' she said with grim satisfaction. 'I just *knew* you'd say that. Well, let me tell you, Liam, the last thing I need at the moment is a speech about your shortcomings. I'm not interested in talking about liability or blame. I want this baby, not because it's my responsibility, but because...because I love it!' She clamped her hand over her trembling lips as her shaking voice became totally suspended by tears.

'Oh, God, Jo.' The anger died from Liam's face leaving a conflict of emotions in its place. 'Can we use the study, Dad?'

'Of course, son. Just you go gently, or you'll have me to answer to,' Pat rumbled stiffly.

Anger flashed in his son's eyes. 'What do you think I am?' Pat lifted one eloquent eyebrow and Liam grated his teeth. 'I get the message. Will you talk to me, Jo?'

Her chin came up to a defiant angle and she glared at him through a sheen of unshed tears. 'If I must,' she muttered ungraciously.

Liam walked straight to the bureau in the study and reached for the half-empty bottle of his father's favourite malt. 'Want one?' he asked. He paused, glass mid-air. 'I forgot...' His eyes touched her middle and he visibly flinched.

'Are you going to get drunk?'

'It hadn't occurred to me, but now you mention it...'

'Well, if you're going to be flippant,' she snapped defensively.

'Flippant,' he said, draining the shallow layer of amber liquid on the bottom of the glass, 'is the last thing I feel. Why the hell didn't you tell me, Jo? You wrote to me about everything else: work, the new wallpaper in your bathroom, your latest cookery class. I suppose it didn't occur to you I might be interested to learn I'm about to be a father.'

She winced at the sarcasm in his voice. 'You seem very sure it's yours. Sure enough to announce it to our joint families,' she reminded him bitterly.

There was a slash of colour across the slope of his sharply defined cheek-bones as he spoke. 'I shouldn't have done that,' he acknowledged reluctantly, 'but to say it was a shock might be the understatement of the century. As for it not being mine, the only other candidate I know of is Justin Wood, and the man isn't capable of making that sort of mistake. He's got the spontaneity of a computer.'

His sneering evaluation made her blood boil. 'Pardon me if I don't share your disdain for caution under the circumstances.'

Liam's head went back as though she'd struck him. 'I don't make a habit of acting so recklessly,' he grated from between clenched teeth.

Jo gave a sigh; this was getting them nowhere. 'I know that, Liam,' she said, wiping the back of her hand across her brow and feeling the light sheen of perspiration there. 'Will you stop pacing? It's making me dizzy.'

He was acting like a caged animal and that was probably what he felt like. Maybe one day Liam would reach the point in his life when he wanted to think about families and stability, but this wasn't that point. I don't want an unwilling captive, Liam, she wanted to say.

'I'm the father.' His blue eyes didn't waver from hers as he sat down beside her on the old leather chesterfield.

She nodded solemnly and willed the emotional tears not to fall. 'Don't do that,' she pleaded, wincing as the flexed joints of his interlocked fingers snapped. He looked at her blankly. 'You'll get arthritis.' She reached out and touched his hand.

A faint movement of his lips disturbed the solemnity of his expression as he regarded her small hand against his darker skin. 'Sounds like an old wives' tale rather than scientific fact to me, Jo.'

'Don't knock old wives, they knew a thing or two.' He turned his hands and her own were sandwiched between his. She looked up, startled. 'I'm sorry I didn't tell you, Liam.' The words came pouring out. 'I wanted to, but it's not the sort of thing you can add as a postscript to a letter, is it?' Her eyes begged his understanding of the situation she'd found herself in. 'What could you have done?

There's no way I would have had an abortion. Whichever way you look at it this is my problem, not yours.'

Her first instinct had been to call him. All she'd wanted was his arms around her, his telling her it would be all right, as he'd done innumerable times at crisis points in the past. It hadn't really mattered that it wouldn't be true this time. Liam was the person she *always* ran to when she was in trouble. It had taken a lot of self-control not to pick up the phone or, better still, catch the first plane.

The transitory softening of Liam's features was replaced by hard anger as she announced her view of the situation. 'And do you think I'd have asked you to have an abortion? Is that the sort of man you think I am, Jo?' He shook his head slowly in disbelief.

'It was never an option so it doesn't really matter what I think,' she faltered under the weight of his anger.

'It sure as hell matters to me!'

'Liam, you're hurting me.'

Liam looked down and was surprised to see her small, delicate hand still ruthlessly crushed between his fingers. 'Sorry.' He was breathing hard, his chest rising and falling steeply, as he released her. 'I won't let you shut me out, Jo.'

'Whatever made you think I'd try?' she responded immediately. 'Of course this is your child, and he or she will know it, and know you, Liam. My friendship with you has always been one of the most important things in my life,' she said, her voice husky with emotion. 'But we have to be practical. We didn't plan this. You didn't *want* to become a father, at least not to *my* child.' The pain was sharp, and it went surprisingly deep, but she continued in a composed voice.

'I know we can't pretend it didn't happen any more, but equally we can't pretend we're suddenly in love.' She gave a sad smile. 'Even if it would make your mother a deliriously happy woman. I'm not trying to sideline you at all, Liam, only it's not *your* body that's involved in all this.' She placed a protective hand over her belly. 'There's a limit to what you can do.'

Despite all these flawlessly logical arguments, Liam found himself unexpectedly assailed by a nagging sense of dissatisfaction. 'You can't do it all alone.'

Jo shrugged. 'People do, and with a lot less family support than I have.'

'What about after the…after the…?'

'Birth?' she suggested. She watched him shake his head as though the idea still seemed incredible to him. 'Don't worry,' she said kindly, 'you'll get used to the idea.' Liam shot her a strange look. 'I did,' she continued. 'I'm healthy and there's no reason I can't work right up to the last minute. Afterwards I've arranged to share a nanny—a three-way split, really, with friends of mine.'

'You've really got this all worked out, haven't you?' He was looking at her as if he'd never actually seen her before.

'Burying my head in the sand was never an option, Liam.'

'Didn't it occur to you I might want to help with the baby, afterwards?'

'*You?*' Laughter was a welcome release really from all the tension. 'S…sorry—' she hiccoughed '—we've got to be realistic here, Liam. Your lifestyle isn't exactly conducive to child-rearing. You can't just transport a baby around like hand baggage; there's a bit more to it than that.'

'I'm aware of that.'

'All right, there's no need to get huffy. One day you'll

meet someone you'll *want* to have a baby with. Maybe I will too.' It could be that paragon did exist somewhere.

'You've become an expert on the subject suddenly, then?' he snarled rather unpleasantly.

'I've read a lot.'

'Ah, *read*,' he drawled sarcastically. 'My sister had read a lot,' he recalled. 'She threw her library in the bin when Liam was six months. Babies trash plans.'

Trust him to zero in on her unspoken doubts and fears. 'I'm flexible.'

'Flexible enough to hold down a job that gives you the social life of a nun?' he enquired sceptically. 'Isn't it this year they promised you a partnership? Wasn't that why you lost the inestimable Justin? You couldn't spare enough time to polish his ego, how the hell are you going to look after a baby?'

'Well, even nuns have nights off— I've got some fairly conclusive proof of that!'

Liam's eyes closed and he struck his forehead with his clenched fist. 'Oh, Jo, what have I done to you? Your career, your plans. I know how hard you've worked.'

'I was there too, remember.' Passive she had *not* been.

'Yes, as a matter of fact I do.'

Under the relentless scrutiny of his direct, unblinking gaze she found her throat closing as simultaneously her limbs grew heavy and totally uncooperative. At least I'm sitting down—falling in a heap would have given rise to unhealthy speculation.

'There's no point crying over spilt milk,' she concluded with painfully false cheerfulness.

'A novel euphemism.'

'There's no need to be snide and clever, Liam. We made a mistake, that's what it all boils down to. I'm not going to let this baby suffer for that.'

'A mistake.' She couldn't understand the bitterness in his deep voice.

'Well, it wasn't as if we intended such a tangible result of our...our...' She chewed on her lower lip and evinced a sudden and deep interest in the ugly print of a pheasant on the wall behind his head.

'Words fail me too,' he said, unexpectedly coming to her aid. 'And that's a problem I don't normally have,' he admitted frankly.

'No, you always have had a lot to say for yourself,' she agreed huskily. Could it be that Liam had been less successful than she'd imagined at wiping out the memory?

'How did your dad take it, Jo?'

'He thinks this wouldn't have happened if Mum had still been alive.' She sighed as a frown formed on her smooth brow. 'It seems everyone feels responsible for me. I'm not stupid, I've thought about the difficulties of combining a career with being a single parent, but the bottom line is you and everyone else will have to abide by my decisions, Liam.'

'This doesn't have to be a battle, Jo.' Uneasily she saw that his expression suggested he'd be prepared to participate if that was what it took.

'That's what I thought,' she said wistfully. That had been before she'd witnessed firsthand his reaction to the news. Given his head, Liam would take the whole affair out of her hands, and she wasn't going to have that!

'I just want to support you.' The scepticism on her face made his teeth jar together. 'You're not alone now.'

'I don't think Suzanna would be happy hearing you say that.'

'Suzanna?'

'The same Suzanna your letters have been full of for the last month.' A female that *perfect* could not have slipped his mind so suddenly. They'd always discussed their partners quite frankly, and it had never bothered her before that he'd had a lot more to discuss than she had, but then she'd never been pregnant before, which probably accounted for the intense dislike she felt for this unknown paragon of womanly virtues.

'Oh, *that* Suzanna.'

The self-conscious flush probably meant it was serious. I'm glad for him, she decided virtuously. 'It might complicate matters if she knows you're a prospective father,' she remarked drily.

'Hell, Jo, I still can't believe it,' Liam said hoarsely.

Jo observed his slightly unfocused expression with sympathy. 'It takes time,' she admitted. He looked as though he was still in shock, and she could readily relate to that.

'Are you well? I mean, is everything all right?' His eyes went to the non-existent bulge of her stomach.

'I'm not very big, am I?' She sighed. 'But the doctor says things are progressing normally.'

'I meant how are *you*?'

'I'm still throwing up, and I seem to need fourteen hours' sleep a night. But other than that...'

'God, no wonder Dad and Uncle Bill looked at me like I'd just crawled out from under a stone.'

'I expect your reputation as a moral crusader can stand it.'

Liam gritted his teeth. 'I'm not talking about my reputation. I'm thinking about what you've been through alone!' he bellowed. 'What is it with you? Why are you determined to paint me as some lightweight incapable of accepting responsibility?'

'Blame it on my hormones—I do. They got me into this mess so I might as well get some mileage out of them,' she quipped a bit nervously. He was taking this even more badly than she'd anticipated.

'*I* got you into this mess, as my father and yours will no doubt point out.'

She frowned. 'I hope you're not going to suggest anything stupid like getting married,' she said suspiciously. 'I'm prepared to make a lot of sacrifices for this baby, but there are limitations!'

There was a pause as Liam looked at her with a peculiar expression in his eyes. 'In some quarters I'm considered quite a catch,' he responded finally.

She gave a relieved laugh—at least he hadn't totally lost his sense of humour. 'Yes, but I know you a lot better than they do,' she pointed out reasonably. 'I'm so glad you're going to be sensible.'

'Sensible?' he said in an odd voice. 'Because I'm not proposing to you?'

'That would be disastrous, wouldn't it?' She wrinkled up her small nose. 'I know platonic marriages based on friendship are meant to work very well, but I want a bit of...fire in mine. If I ever have one.'

'Well, I hope you're not relying on Justin Wood to supply the spark, Jo, because I'd say he's the flame-resistant type.' Unaccountably he looked extremely angry.

'I don't know what you've got against Justin,' she responded crossly.

'And I don't know what you see in him! Never have done. I don't know what you're defending him for—he's the one who gave you the push after...how long did this *passionate* affair go on for?'

'You're well aware I went out with Justin for two years. How would you like it if I criticised your girlfriends?'

'And I suppose it wasn't criticism when you suggested Tania's figure owed more to silicone than nature?'

'Which one was she? I forget. I know some people might say you lack staying power, but I—'

'You have the tongue of a viper.' The reluctant smile died from his face as he slipped off the sofa and knelt down beside her. 'This is one situation you can't joke yourself out of, Jo.' He caught her hands firmly within his. 'You feel like ice,' he observed with a frown as he began to rub her fingers to restore circulation. 'I think we've got to come to some sort of formal arrangement concerning the baby.'

'Why does it have to be formal?' For a minute there when he'd gone down on his knees she'd thought...! Ridiculous. Liam wouldn't be stupid enough to even suggest it. She had seen the way he'd reacted when his mother had mentioned the word 'marriage'. His horror at the very thought had been apparent in that unguarded moment.

'The idea of my child being brought up by a Justin clone makes my blood run cold,' he said frankly.

Jo pulled her hands free of his crossly. 'The implication being, you don't trust me to put the interests of my child first.'

'Our child,' he reminded her.

Jo gave a frustrated sigh. 'I wish I'd never told you.' Life was complicated enough already without having a possessive father to contend with. The fact that what he said made sense didn't help at all.

'You didn't!' he reminded her, and she flushed under his ironic gaze and then went very pale. 'I don't want to pressure you.' Unexpectedly he took her face in his hands. For a second she thought he was going to kiss her; his eyes were certainly lingering overlong on the full curve of her mouth. Her heart was thudding so loud he could probably feel the vibrations. 'I'll even break it to Mum there won't be wedding bells.' With a lopsided smile he released her.

'Good luck.' She was glad he hadn't sealed their tentative bargaining with a kiss. Relief made her feel quite nauseous for a moment and she didn't dare risk getting to her feet until her knees had stopped shaking.

CHAPTER TWO

'YOU'LL get those lovely shiny shoes dirty if you come in here,' Jo warned. The sight of the long legs attached to those shoes instantly put an end to a peaceful half-hour during which she'd managed not to think about anything taxing. She took her time straightening up to give her racing heart time to slow. 'I'm feeding Napoleon.'

For a man who often bemoaned the fact that his clients could be sentimental about their animals, Bill Smith often brought home a selection of waifs and strays—occasionally one was just too unappealing or antisocial to be found a permanent home. Napoleon, a particularly vile-tempered billy-goat was one of this number, a permanent fixture for many years now.

'A man could be excused for thinking you didn't want me near you.' He kept a wary eye on the goat. 'That animal has never liked me.'

She couldn't have asked for a more innocuous conversation; there was certainly nothing in his manner to explain her tumultuous pulse-rate and shaky knees.

'Normally I'd say you shouldn't endow animals with human characteristics, but in this case... I'll tie him up—the bill might be hefty if he decides to eat that rather smart suit.' Loose Italian styling in dark grey made him appear almost a stranger. 'We don't usually dress for Sunday lunch,' she joked, to cover her growing confusion.

'I don't think I'm invited,' Liam responded drily. 'Your dad told me you were here.' One dark brow quirked meaningfully. 'I've a meeting, in Manchester,' he added, casually smoothing down his silk tie.

Jo put down the plastic bucket and, hands thrust in the pockets of her jeans, she stepped out into the weak morning sunlight. 'You've seen Dad, then. Was it *very* awful?'

'You could say we had a frank exchange of views. His view being that I'm a selfish, untrustworthy bastard who has taken advantage of his hospitality by seducing his daughter.'

She winced whilst acknowledging privately it could have been worse. Dad's language the previous night had been a lot less restrained. 'I'm sorry, Liam, but he's a bit upset right now.'

'I didn't say I disagreed with him.'

'Don't you start,' she snapped. 'I've had enough of that nonsense from him! I told Dad if anyone did the seducing it was me!' Unpalatable though it might be, this was a fact and she couldn't pretend it wasn't. Chin tilted, she dared him to contradict her.

Something flickered at the back of his eyes. 'That must have gone down well. I'm surprised he didn't turn the dogs on me.'

Jo smiled a little wanly as she thought of her father's motley collection of other people's rejects—one thing they all had in common was extreme docility. 'If he had they might have drooled you to death. Do you remember when—?'

'We need to do some serious talking, Jo.' His expression made it clear he didn't share her desire to reminisce. 'You can't act as though nothing has changed.'

He's telling *me* that! 'You prefer Greek tragedy? I'll polish up my heart-rending sobs, shall I? You don't have to tell *me* nothing is ever going to be the same—I've worked that out even hampered by my limited intelligence.'

He reached out and placed a hand on her shoulder. 'Point taken, Jo. You just seem so...so calm about all this.'

She had to smile at that. He had no notion of the blind panic that had seized her when she'd first realised she was pregnant. 'Your life doesn't have to change fundamentally because of this.' It was only natural he'd be concerned—having fatherhood thrust upon him was bound to be an unsettling experience.

His fingers tightened over the curve of her collar-bone and she winced. 'Sorry,' he grated, dropping his arm. 'You're assuming I couldn't cope with the demands of fatherhood.'

The anger emanating from his tense body confused her. 'I'm sure you could cope, I'm just saying you don't have to. I'll be fine on my own...' The blast of fury from his blue eyes made her voice trail away.

'Only you won't be on your own, you'll have *my* child.' She suddenly realised she'd been naive not to expect this possessiveness, but it genuinely hadn't occurred to her.

'And the child will have you too, but not on a full-time basis. That's all I was trying to say.' Considering the obvious depth of his feeling she was prepared to overlook his hostility.

'But you'll grant me visitation rights.'

'We won't need anything like that,' she said, shocked by his suggestion and the bitterness in his tone.

'You say that now, but what about later when a new Justin is back on the scene? Has it ever occurred to you that I don't want to be a part-time father?'

What was he saying? They both knew nothing else was possible. She couldn't believe this was Liam talking; he was like a stranger—a stranger, furthermore, she didn't much like. 'You're talking nonsense.'

'I'm making a valid point. I'm not prepared to leave the future to take care of itself, not when it's my child we're talking about.'

'Our child,' she said quietly.

'Pardon?'

'Our child,' she said, her voice moving swiftly up the scales. 'You keep saying *my* child this, *my* child that. I am involved in this,' she reminded him sarcastically. 'What a fool I was to assume that this would be easier because we're friends! If I had to have a one-night stand I wish I'd had it with a stranger! It would have made things a lot easier.'

Under his tan Liam went white and the vivid colour of his eyes seemed more pronounced by contrast. 'We're all wise in retrospect. It would seem you're stuck with me as the father of your child, Jo. You'd better come to terms with the fact I'm not about to disappear.'

'Not even to Manchester,' she reminded him. 'If we're talking priorities…' She could see from his expression that her jibe had hit home.

'I *have* to go,' he bit back. 'If I could avoid it I would. I know the timing stinks, but I'll be back tomorrow and we'll talk.'

'I'll be at work tomorrow.'

'Stay here and wait for me.'

He had a very elegant way of moving, but Jo was in no mood to appreciate the aesthetic beauty of his retreating back. Maybe Liam was accustomed to people jumping when he started flinging his orders about, but he'd discover she wasn't one of them. Wait here for me indeed!

'Thanks, Justin, you don't have to do this, you know.'

'Despite the way things turned out, Jo, I hope we can still be civilised,' he replied rather stiffly. But then Justin, she reflected, never had been a casual person.

'I'm really grateful,' she said warmly as he stacked the books she passed him into a packing case. She looked around the half-empty office with sad eyes. To her mind her personal imprint was already vanishing from the small room along with the pot plants and books.

'I wish you'd let me speak to my colleague about unfair dismissal proceedings,' he said with a disapproving frown. 'It's all most irregular—you deserve compensation.' His legal brain disliked seeing her waste an opportunity for recompense. 'I'd represent you myself, but it's not my field.'

Jo was touched by his offer. 'No, I've thought about it and I don't want to,' she said firmly. 'Besides, they were very careful *not* to say, We're sacking you because single parents aren't good for the image of MacGrew and Bartnett,' she recalled bitterly. No, it had been all exquisitely polite. 'There was only ever a verbal agreement that I'd be offered the partnership this year—you know that, Justin. They didn't actually sack me—I could have accepted a demotion.'

'But they knew you wouldn't.'

The shake of her head conceded this. It hadn't mattered to her four years ago that she'd been taken on as a token female in the well-known, but deeply conservative, firm of accountants. She had been given an opportunity to show how good she was at competing with the very best. She'd thrived on the competition.

Up until now it had seemed her tactics had paid off, she'd made her mark. She'd been so good for business that

she had been unofficially told she was about to be offered
a partnership. At twenty-seven, she would be the youngest
partner they'd ever had. That was until she'd been sum-
moned into the boardroom that morning. A 'reduction in
her workload' was the way they'd put it.

'Well, I think their whole attitude belongs in the Dark
Ages,' Justin said sternly.

Despite her simmering anger and sense of injustice, Jo
almost smiled. She'd never imagined she'd see the day
when the ultra-conventional Justin would side with con-
temporary morality. Despite his looks, which made him
appear rather dangerous and dashing, he really was an old-
fashioned traditionalist at heart. In reality he was only dangerous in a court of law, where, by all accounts he was a
ruthless litigator. Justin was a classic example of the well-
tried maxim 'Don't judge a book by the cover', she reflected.

She cursed as the pile of papers she was carrying slipped
to the floor. She dropped to her knees and began gathering
them up. Justin joined her; she was rather surprised he was
risking getting dust on his immaculate pinstriped trousers.
Justin took a great deal of pride in his appearance and she
doubted he ever wore anything that hadn't been exclu-
sively tailormade for him.

'I can't understand how you're being so calm. When I
suggested we get married, your work was the reason you
gave for turning me down. Now just a few months later
here you are jobless...pregnant.'

Barefoot and starving, she silently added. 'Thanks,
Justin, it had slipped my mind,' she responded drily.

'I thought giving you an ultimatum, walking out, would
bring you to your senses. I never thought...' He shook his
head in disbelief. 'It didn't even occur to me this would

happen. *I* wanted a child, it was you who said you weren't ready,' he accused, his voice thickening.

'I'm so sorry, Justin.' Recognising the depth of his feeling, she touched his shoulder. She'd never actually thought he'd take his moral blackmail to its logical conclusion, and when he had she'd been devastated.

Justin looked at her hand. 'Things could have been so different,' he said, covering her hand with his.

'Oh, Justin!' What could she say? She hadn't been able to commit herself to a more formal alliance even to save their relationship. The sense of loss was still there, but time had given her a fresh perspective on the situation and she found she could hardly recall the raw emotions of their traumatic parting now.

I must be shallow and fickle, she concluded miserably. What she'd felt for Justin had just never been going to lead anywhere; her feelings had been too superficial. She could hardly believe now she'd been so traumatised.

'I wish it was my baby you were carrying, darling.'

I don't, Jo realised guiltily. The strength of her certainty came as something of a shock.

'Well, it isn't, mate, it's mine.' Liam was watching the tender scene with a distinctly jaundiced eye.

'Liam, what are you doing here?' This guilt thing was getting rather tiresome.

'The question is what are *you* doing here? I thought we arranged to meet back home this morning!'

'*You* arranged,' she told him pointedly. 'I can't put my life on hold while I wait for you to put in an appearance.'

'From what I hear, your life, at least professionally, has been put on hold. Couldn't you just do *nothing* until I got back? Have you really handed in your notice?'

'Call me peculiar, but I don't feel I'm cut out to be the

office junior,' she snapped back, placing her sheaf of papers back on the desktop.

'They made it that obvious?'

'It's constructive dismissal.' Jo was grateful for Justin's intervention; the last thing she felt like doing was explaining the whole saga yet again.

'I didn't ask you! What's he doing here anyway?' Liam asked Jo belligerently after dismissing Justin with a sneer. 'And what sort of idiot lets a pregnant woman go heaving around packing cases?'

'How dare you talk to Justin like that?' she gasped incredulously. 'I know you're not exactly happy about the situation, but it doesn't give you the right to abuse my friends. For your information I asked Justin to help me.' This wasn't strictly true but Liam needed putting in his place with a firm hand.

Justin stood up, flicked an imaginary speck of dust off his dark trousers and straightened the rose in his lapel. 'I expect Jo was looking to her more *reliable* friends.'

This blatant provocation took Jo's breath away and she suspected Justin might be regretting it too. Liam was looking quite simply murderous. Broad-shouldered and lean-hipped, his long-legged frame was physically intimidating, she had to admit. The black leather jacket, white tee shirt and jeans he wore served to emphasise the stark contrast between the two men. Whilst it might have been Justin's looks which had initially attracted her, it had been the undemanding nature of their relationship which had kept them together. By comparison Liam was a *very* demanding and unreasonable sort of man.

Liam topped Justin's six feet by several inches. They were both dark-haired but there the similarity ended. Liam's hair wasn't nicely trimmed, it was thick and silky, inclined to wave and at the moment touched his collar. She knew the length and lack of style weren't a fashion statement, he just habitually forgot to keep hair appointments. Liam had the same olive colouring as his father and, with his rather prominent nose and thick, slanted eyebrows, he had none of Justin's smooth good looks. What he did have in abundance was sex appeal—buckets of the stuff.

'You sound like you have something to say, Wood. Don't stop,' Liam drawled, 'I'm fascinated.'

Jo pulled at the collar of her silk shirt with a hint of desperation. The air-conditioned room was suddenly stifling. Why had she never noticed how, well, *noticeable* Liam was before?

'Jo, what's wrong?' Liam's sharp, anxious enquiry seemed to come from a long way off. 'Get out the way, you idiot, she's going to faint.'

'Don't fuss,' she complained weakly as she was firmly laid down on the carpet.

'Stay where you are,' Liam barked. 'You want to let the blood get to your brain—let's face it, it's not that easy to find.' His fingers touched the inner aspect of her clammy wrist where her pulse was lively enough. 'Have you done this before?'

'Done what?' Even when she closed her eyes the black dots still danced across her vision.

'Fainted,' came the impatient reply.

'I've never fainted in my life.'

Liam bent his head to catch her words. 'Give me strength!' Strength didn't seem to be something he lacked as he lifted her up into his arms. 'Get out of the way!' he snapped as he collided with Justin in the doorway.

'You've spilt the water,' Justin complained, empty glass

in hand. 'You can't do that!' he objected sharply as Liam shouldered his way past.

'What is it I can't do?'

'Abduct her.'

'Grow up, man!' Liam recommended tersely. 'I'm quite happy to exchange pleasantries with you at a time of your choosing.'

Pistols at dawn, my seconds will call on yours, Jo thought, swallowing an inappropriate giggle.

'Only right now Jo needs to get out of this place.' She saw him dismiss the small space she'd worked so hard for with a fastidious sneer before he strode off leaving Justin staring after him, a frustrated expression on his red face.

Justin wouldn't do anything as undignified as chase after them, she knew that. *He* certainly wouldn't have made a spectacle of himself by carrying her through the heart of the plush building.

'Poor Justin.' It obviously hadn't occurred to Liam to do anything as obvious as ask her whether she required being rescued—dragged off like a sack of flour. Finesse never had been one of his more striking traits.

Liam snorted. 'Poor Justin, my foot! He couldn't wait to get out of the room when things went pear-shaped back there.'

There was a spot just between his shoulder and the angle of his square jaw that could have been created for the specific use of supporting her aching head. 'He's not very good with illness—not that I'm ill.'

'If you'd told me that earlier I wouldn't have caused untold injury to my back.'

Even though she was still angry with him, she laughed weakly. 'I could probably walk now.'

'Don't spoil it, Jo, I'm quite enjoying myself,' he confided against her ear. 'All these years wasted perfecting my modern man technique,' he complained. 'Modern man, my foot! These women go a bundle on the caveman style. I've never been on the receiving end of so many come-hither looks in my life! Women never fail to amaze me!'

'Glad to be of service. Who are you planning to drag off to your cave?' Who was he kidding? He was *always* on the receiving end of come-hither looks. The resignation with which she generally viewed the peculiar tastes of her fellow females seemed to have deserted her for the moment.

'Your cave seems the best destination.'

'My keys are in my bag, which is in the office—we'll have to go back.' The thought of backtracking and being the focus of all those curious eyes again made her cringe.

'I've got a key, remember. If I go back in there I'll probably throttle that overdressed, self-opinionated bore.'

'What a trusting soul I was to give you a key,' she said wearily.

'Meaning what, exactly? It works both ways, remember: you've got my key. Do you want to sit in the front or lie in the back?' he asked as they reached the underground car park. He placed her carefully on the floor and unlocked the four-wheel drive he drove.

'I'm not an invalid,' she snapped, displaying her independence by climbing into the front seat. 'And what I mean is, I had watering my plants in mind when I handed over the key, not assaulting my friends. You've been watching too many Rambo movies.'

He started up the engine. 'If life was as simple as it is in action movies I'd be a happy man,' he admitted, with a lamentable lack of shame for his ludicrous behaviour. 'There are roadworks at the junction so make yourself comfortable, it'll be a long ride. You told Wood I'm the father?' His eyes flickered to her face.

Sensational, thrillingly blue eyes that were part of his Celtic heritage. She'd never associated sensational and thrilling with Liam's eyes before. She suddenly experienced a deep longing to step back in time and have their relationship back on its smooth, familiar footing.

'Before your dramatic announcement, you mean? Yes, I did.' Just as well—the poor man would probably have had an apoplexy if he'd first learnt the truth that brutally. 'I think I owed Justin the truth after all we've had together.'

Liam's nostrils flared and he made a sound of disgust.

'Does it bother you he knows? Is it meant to be a secret?' she shouted, her indignation rising at his sneering response.

Jo saw the flicker of anger in his eyes as he shot her a swift sideways glance. 'It seems I was the only one not in on the secret—he probably knew before me,' he accused thickly. 'Forgive my confusion but I'm obviously out of date. The last time you spoke about Justin, he'd broken your heart. Or don't you remember the occasion?'

'I'm hardly likely to forget, am I?'

'Neither am I, Jo.' The inflection in his deep voice sent the colour flaring in her cheeks. 'You didn't tell me he wanted to marry you.'

'No.' She'd been distracted. Had he forgotten, or was he remembering what she *had* said that night?

The possibility that he was recalling the same things she was made the fine, downy hair on her forearms stand on end. A shiver slithered slowly down her spine as, dry-mouthed, she risked a swift look in his direction from under the sheltering sweep of her eyelashes.

He'd come hotfoot in response to her tearful phone call when Justin had walked out on her. She'd been too absorbed by her own misery to register the lines of exhaustion bracketing his mouth and the tell-tale shadow on his jaw. He'd held her whilst she'd wept, murmuring soothing nothings in appropriate places, sliding his fingers tenderly through her damp hair, pushing the tangled strands off her hot forehead and gently patting her back. When the storm hadn't abated his lips had replaced his fingers on her damp cheeks, across her forehead, the tip of her nose.

Finally, when her sobs had subsided, she'd given an exhausted sigh. 'What would I do without you?' His tenderness brought a lump of emotion to her throat and made her voice husky. She put all the gratitude, warmth and love that filled her heart to overflowing into the kiss she pressed on his lips.

The sudden tension in him communicated itself to her immediately. Had she offended him? 'I'm sorry...' she began, suddenly horribly afraid she'd overstepped some invisible boundary.

His blue eyes were burning with a strange light. She was ill prepared for the sudden weakness that pervaded her limbs—it went bone-deep. His glance flickered to the bare curve of her right shoulder, exposed where the baggy neck of her nightshirt had slipped. A sharp, painful sound swiftly cut off emerged from his chest.

Holding her upturned face, his thumbs running down the length of her jaw, he bent closer. Like a sleepwalker he repeated her own impulsive action exactly. It should have been chaste, clinical even, their lips were modestly closed. It wasn't!

Frantic! When he lifted his mouth from hers she felt *frantic*. It couldn't stop! He had to do that again, surely he could see that too? Through half-closed eyes she tried to read the hard lines and angles of his face.

His laugh grated on her sensitised nerve-endings. 'Feel better now?' He wasn't reading the right page of the script. She shook her head in a gesture of denial; this wasn't the time for prosaic words.

She felt a spurt of anger as he ruffled her hair, a need to lash out. Why must he always treat her like a child?

'Do *you* feel better?' she enquired in open challenge. She didn't even try to understand the compulsion which drove her.

She couldn't plead error in retrospect; it was quite deliberate when her hands moved under the hem of his shirt. Fingers spread, palms flat, she slowly slid her hands up over his flat, tight belly and higher still to the muscle-packed expanse of his chest. *Nothing*, she decided, could feel better than his warm, satiny skin—the texture was intoxicating. The deep shudder that rippled through his immobile form must have involved every muscle in his body.

'What do you think you're doing?'

If his voice had been icily cold it might have doused the fire in her brain, but it wasn't—it held a husky rasp that made her tremble even harder. Tremble, yes, I am, she realised, feeling oddly objective about this discovery.

'We both know what I'm doing, Liam.' Her voice was husky but incredibly calm. Calm was the last thing she felt, she felt reckless, and drunk on power. 'It's what I'll do next that's got me wondering.'

'You're not yourself.'

'You've no idea what a relief that is.' Herself was miserable, depressed...repressed, a small voice added.

'You don't know what you're doing.'

'I know that these buttons are hellish difficult. Could you help…?'

He caught her wrists then, roughly, and pulled them away from his body. 'Don't play games.'

This had to be the most humiliating moment of her life! 'Don't look at me as if I'm an axe murderer! All I want is a kiss. If it's too much trouble, don't bother!' she yelled, feeling totally mortified. She tossed her head and ripped her hands from his grasp. She held only a tenuous hope of salvaging even a shred of pride.

She didn't get more than a step away before he reached her and, with one arm around her waist, lifted her feet off the ground. The impetus of his action as he turned her around drove them forwards until her back was against the wall. The breath was driven from her body.

Her head dropped forward. No wonder he was angry. She was acting like some sort of…of sex-starved tart. His hands were on her shoulders and she could feel his nearness from the heat of his body. She was too ashamed to look at him.

'I'm sorry, don't hate me…' Her voice cracked.

'Hate? Oh, God, Jo, I could never, no, don't cry again, darling. I know you're feeling rejected; the bastard, I'd like to kill Justin,' he said viciously. 'You don't need to indulge in casual sex to prove you're desirable.' She wanted to deny this analysis but he kissed the corner of her mouth, then the other corner. 'I know you don't believe me, but you'll be better off without him.'

She did shake her head in denial this time, and the next kiss hit dead centre. He pulled back, but only a fraction. Jo opened her eyes; she still had her eyes open when they moved forward simultaneously. Her lips parted and there was only a momentary delay before he accepted her offer.

He didn't just accept it, he took the initiative out of her hands in a big way. She'd never experienced anything that came close to the onslaught of his lips and tongue as his teeth tugged and nipped, his tongue tasted and explored. Her body was filled with a languorous heat, her senses swam, she *ached*!

'This is crazy!' The groaned words were wrenched from him. He might have acknowledged insanity, but that didn't stop his lips from continuing to strain hungrily against hers. His hands slipped to her hips barely covered by the plain cotton nightshirt she wore. The contact made her body jerk.

'That's lovely, don't stop,' she begged throatily. Lovely, exciting, sizzlingly erotic, it was all that and more! Jo had never felt so primitively aroused in her life. As her feet left the floor she instinctively wrapped her legs around his waist. She arched her back and provocatively pressed her slim, lithe body as close to him as possible.

'Your skin's so soft, so smooth.' His tongue strayed over the graceful curve of her collar-bone for a moment and she whimpered with delirious pleasure.

Blindly, panting hard, Liam reached behind her for the door. More luck than judgement brought their erratic progress, interrupted as it was by gasps and moans as each new sensation was explored and enjoyed, to her narrow bed. He fell with her onto the bed, impressing her body into the soft mattress.

Her trailing arm sent the bedside light crashing onto the floor. 'It doesn't matter,' she said as he lifted his head. She didn't want to illuminate the scene, she didn't want anything to intrude on the unreal quality of this incredible episode. Dark was safer.

If she paused long enough to think that it was *Liam* who

was pulling her nightshirt over her head, and Liam whose tongue was tasting every inch of her aching breasts, it would spoil everything. She'd be left with the paradox of why she wanted—no, why she *needed* him to.

His need was as great as hers, even through the layers of his clothes she could feel that. He was in the grip of a desire just as blind as the one which drove her to rip at his shirt and curse softly with frustration as her fingers fumbled over the buckle of his belt.

When he took control of that problem she encouraged or very possibly distracted him with soft kisses pressed on the strong curve of his back. He lay back down and she eagerly insinuated herself closer to him, only to be momentarily thrown off her stride when he sat up again, laughing.

'What?' If he changed his mind now the consequences might well be fatal!

'I've still got my boots on.' Faint laughter still rumbled in the vault of his chest.

Laughter was rapidly replaced by frantic murmurs when he returned to her. Imprisoned by his heavy, hair-roughened thighs, her nostrils filled with the warm, masculine, aroused scent of his body, she lost what little control she had and every inhibition that had ever restrained her.

She wanted to taste him, touch him, and she did so with joyous abandon. The strength of his body and its eye-opening muscularity delighted her. He guided her forays with a firm hand, and in his turn touched her until her harsh gasps echoed in the dark room.

Over the years, she knew, he'd had enough practice at such things, but there was nothing slick or polished about him now. His responses were raw, his elegant, strong hands shook and his body trembled as though he were struggling against an invisible barrier. The next day her body bore the marks of his urgent caresses.

Waking at some point in the night, Jo's mind instantly went into replay mode. The culmination of their wild, unrestrained coupling had resulted in an equally violent release. Sleepily, she tried to make sense of it. She didn't have a strong sex drive, did she? I actually shouted! She sat up with a jolt. No. *'I screamed!'* In the darkness the blush spread over her body.

Her action in the confined space sent the quilt slithering onto the floor. Run or retrieve the quilt? Not a complex decision, but one that taxed her flustered mind at that moment. If she hadn't sat there dithering Liam wouldn't have woken up!

He rolled over onto his side and threw his leg over her hip. The weight of his thigh immobilised her. 'What did you say?' The purr of his deep, sleepy murmur made her tense.

'I didn't say anything.'

'Yes, you did.' He paused, obviously trawling through his sleepy recollections before coming up with the goods. 'You said, "'I screamed."'

'Nonsense.' She tried to pull the rumpled sheet up from the bottom of the bed.

'You did, you know. You said—'

She didn't need reminding of what she'd said, it was branded on her memory. 'Don't!' she shrieked, putting both her hands firmly over what she hoped was his mouth. It was—despite the pressure of her fingers his lips parted and his tongue flickered over the centre of her palm.

She might have denied the words but she couldn't deny the arousing quality of the damp touch. It was ridiculous but all the strength left her body in a silent whoosh. She fell forward and put her hands out to cushion her fall. It was all part of the weird conspiracy that Liam found her hands had been replaced by the soft contours of her breasts. It wasn't an exchange he appeared to have any problems with.

'A gift from the gods,' he murmured as his mouth closed around one swollen rosy peak. His actions no longer had the raw urgency of earlier, but as she lay, her body spread-eagled over his, she couldn't doubt the strength of his arousal.

She moaned and tried to raise herself up on her elbows. 'We can't do this.'

Liam's hands came up to cover the curve of her buttocks, his thumbs hooked around the angle of her hipbones. 'Actually, it wouldn't be that difficult and there's a strong possibility it would be pleasurable.' Her breath caught sharply as his tongue unexpectedly traced the still damp area of her nipple. 'You are so sensitive it's incredible, especially there.'

'Everywhere.' With you, anyway, she realised in bewilderment.

The whispered admission brought a deep purr of male satisfaction from his throat. 'Then I'll have to be very attentive. You'll have to tell me if there's anywhere I miss.'

'You can't say things like that to me.'

'Why, don't you like to hear them?' The taunting quality in his deep, caressing tones made her throat ache. Her body was taut and trembling with anticipation so she couldn't immediately allow herself to accept. Excitement was building inside her until she couldn't breathe.

'You're sorry for me.'

'Lust isn't pity.'

'Is this lust?' He tugged her down until her face was level with his, her breasts were crushed against his chest and her knees were either side of his thighs.

'Does it need to have a name,' he groaned, 'when it feels so good? You smell of me. You taste of me.' His open mouth moved over her neck. He obviously found the discovery exciting—his body surged suggestively against her.

'I want to...'

'What, sweetheart? What do you want to do to me?' His breath was warm and fragrant on her cheek. His hands moved slowly, sensuously over her back, down the curve of her thigh. He flexed her knee and ran his thumb over the sensitive skin of her instep. 'If I tell you what I like, will it help?'

Every wicked, honeyed syllable was fraying the edges of her doubts and inhibitions until they snapped. 'I want...I want to do everything to you,' she half sobbed. 'And I want you to do everything to me.'

That was the end of her resistance and the beginning—the beginning of an experience that was infinitely more intimate than their earlier frantic encounter. A slow, sensuous voyage of discovery where the power of the word was as great as the power of taste and touch.

And *such words*—she couldn't think now about the things she'd said without her skin burning. She hadn't even suspected that the male mind could contain such erotic fantasies—she ought to have been shocked, but each velvet syllable that had dripped like honey from his lips had aroused her to even greater heights of passion.

'I've been thinking.'

Totally disorientated, she blinked and tried to focus her

glazed vision. Her own thoughts had absorbed her so deeply she couldn't immediately respond.

'Are you all right?' he persisted.

'Yes, fine.'

'You looked a bit strange there for a minute.'

'Don't fuss.' Just as well I wasn't in the driver's seat, she reflected grimly. It isn't healthy, this constant preoccupation with an incident best forgotten. What's wrong with me? It was a one-off—well, two-off to be accurate— the result of a freak set of circumstances, nothing more. Forget it ever happened, wasn't that what Liam had said? He'd only slept with her out of pity, she reminded herself.

'I've been thinking.'

So have I! 'So you keep saying. Are you going to share it?'

'I think we should get married after all.'

CHAPTER THREE

THE car drew to a halt. 'Did you hear what I said? You must have considered it too.'

'Must I?' Had Liam gone mad, stark staring mad? He sounded as if he were discussing nothing more emotional than buying a new car.

'It's the obvious solution when you look at things logically.'

'Logic's going to come into this, is it?' Logic had always been the term Liam used when he twisted facts to prove he'd been right all along. Jo gritted her teeth and squared her shoulders. Anger was to be expected—anyone would be angry, but why was this farcical proposal hurting so much?

'We have to be practical.'

'Thanks for sharing your breathtaking insight and wisdom.'

'You can't laugh this situation off,' he said, his expression austere with disapproval.

'I promise you this isn't laughter.' Her bosom swelled with indignation. She winced as the fabric of her light bra chafed her ultra-sensitive nipples. He could offer her advice when *his* bosoms were almost visibly inflating by the hour! If he had bosoms, that was—which he didn't, he had... She felt a confusing surge of warmth as she remembered exactly what he had in their place.

She was relieved when his sober voice interrupted her mental detours. 'I know you like your independence, but a baby will inevitably make inroads into that, and if you have me to support you misfortunes like losing your job needn't become major disasters. I don't think you're being entirely realistic about the future, Jo, are you?' His tolerant, kindly tone made her want to punch him. 'Friendship isn't such a bad basis for marriage. It would make our families happy.'

'So I should marry you to please our families?' she enquired with interest. Anger was building steadily inside her. Was he *trying* to insult her? Did he honestly think that any woman in her right mind would go along with such a crazy—such a *cold* proposition?

'That's not what I was saying,' he interrupted impatiently.

Stay calm, Jo, she told herself as she unbuckled her seat belt. 'Pardon me, Liam, but that's *exactly* what you were saying, in your own uniquely patronising way. I'm sorry Dad won't speak to you. I've tried to reason with him.'

She'd repeatedly told him it wasn't Liam's fault, but her words had made no impact on him at all. When she'd initially refused to discuss the issue of the baby's father he'd brought no pressure to bear. In fact, he'd been incredibly supportive, but now he knew it was Liam his entire attitude had, somewhat unreasonably, changed.

'It's unfair, I know, but I think marriage is a bit of a drastic solution to help you out of an uncomfortable situation.'

'I don't care if Uncle Bill won't speak to me. I don't give a damn if my own father is acting as though he's reared a monster.'

'I didn't know it was that bad.' She grimaced sympathetically. It was obvious he did care, he cared a lot, but that was no excuse for his clinical and impractical solution.

'Dad made his feelings *quite* plain after you left the other night,' Liam said drily. 'That's beside the point.' He shrugged off the rift between him and his father. 'Between us we've created a life, Jo, that's something special. A child needs two parents. You need someone to look after you.'

'Granted, but they don't have to be married to one another.' His words brought an emotional lump to her throat.

'I'm damned if I'll see my child brought up by the likes of Justin Wood!' His expression echoed the repugnance in his words.

'I might have known it! What a hypocrite you are, Liam Rafferty.' She cast him a look of disgust and scrambled out of the vehicle. To think she'd been in danger of getting all misty-eyed and choked. To play on her guilt was a low trick. He had picked his points so cleverly with the sole intention of driving his message home; and to think she'd always admired his straightforward honesty!

'Don't walk away when I'm talking to you,' he yelled, following her.

'All that rubbish about creating a life together and facing up to our responsibilities! Supporting me, my foot!' She gave a snort of disgust as she stamped along. 'You're not concerned about me, you just don't want Justin or any other man being involved in the upbringing of your child. The only person you're considering is yourself,' she flung over her shoulder.

'That's a lie!' His face was dark with anger.

'Don't insult my intelligence. You've never liked any of my boyfriends,' she recalled, 'and as for Justin you've always had your knife into him. All those snide remarks and sly digs. Justin would make a marvellous father.' Her smile glittered with angry malice. 'Yes,' she mused, 'the more I think about it, the more it seems the best solution all round.'

Liam seized her by the shoulders. There was something

primeval about the fury that drew his features into a taut mask. 'I accept you want to punish me for wrecking your life, but don't even think about taking that route,' he said thickly.

She swayed slightly under the impact of his white-hot warning. She'd always known there was a ruthless element in Liam's character, but she'd never experienced it first-hand before—she'd never expected to.

'You don't get it, do you, Liam? My life isn't ruined; I *want* this child.' Something in her expression and the clear, sure sound of her voice penetrated the fog of his anger.

He let her go and took a step backwards. He didn't try to stop her as she walked away.

Jo had never felt so wretched in her life. They'd never had a row before, not a real one—squabbles, yes, but they'd been mended swiftly and left no scars. She'd never *tried* to hurt him before—wanted to hurt him. She rested her head on her knees and pushed her back into the cold surface of the wall.

'Hello.'

Jo surreptitiously wiped her nose with the back of her hand before lifting her head. 'I thought you'd gone.'

Looking at the tear-stained face, Liam swallowed hard. 'So how were you planning to get in?'

She shrugged. 'I hadn't thought about it.'

'Come on, you can't sit there.' He caught her elbow and urged her to her feet. He didn't look angry now, he looked wary and almost as weary as she felt—all this emotional stuff was certainly tiring! She remained silent as he turned the key in the lock. 'I suppose you want this back?' He held out the palm of his hand.

Jo looked at the key. No, it was too symbolic, too final, she wasn't ready to give up on their friendship yet.

'You'd better keep it for emergencies,' she said without looking up at him. Silently he followed her into the small flat.

Normally he'd have breezed into the sitting room after he'd been away, flop down onto her chintzy sofa and demand she put on the kettle. Today he stood there stiff and awkward, like a stranger; it broke her heart to see it.

'Will you tell me the truth if I ask you something, Jo?'

'It depends on the question,' she replied, her thoughts racing. What answer could be that important? What question could make him look so grave?

'Are you *glad* you're pregnant? I don't mean in a philosophical sense, I mean *genuinely* happy.'

She shot him a startled look. 'Yes.'

Deeper than confusion, worry, fear and the inevitable guilt, what she actually felt was a deep contentment. Until he'd actually suggested it she hadn't even considered this facet of the situation.

'I expect that seems strange to you? Maybe it's something to do with my biological clock?' she suggested.

Her biological clock hadn't appeared to be ticking loudly when Justin had very recently suggested it was time they started a family.

'So you wanted to get pregnant.'

'Are you,' she asked incredulously, 'suggesting I *planned* this?'

'Not consciously...' Despite his words Jo could see he was giving the idea serious consideration.

'And naturally I'd choose you as the father.' This was unbelievable!

'Post-mortems aren't going to do us much good.'

Jo had never gone out of her way to disprove the theory that redheads and a placid temperament did not go together, but, even by her tempestuous standards, he could see that she was working herself up into a right royal fury!

The sparks from her narrowed green eyes were a danger to flammable materials. The fiery quality of her red curls served to emphasise her sudden drastic pallor. The idea of such a passionate, elemental creature becoming an accountant of all things had always seemed ironic. He recalled that his laughter when she'd confided her ambitions had made her furious. He'd coaxed away her anger that time—this time he didn't think it would be so easy.

'You're the one trawling my subconscious! You really do think a lot of yourself, don't you, Liam? If I was choosing a father for my child you'd be the *last* person I'd choose. When have you ever stayed in a relationship more than a couple of months?' Hands on hips, she swept her eyes disparagingly over him.

'Your attitude to women hardly screams emotionally mature!' she observed scornfully. 'Your lifestyle makes a gypsy's seem stable. Call me old-fashioned, but I've always thought that in an ideal world it's kind of nice for a child to be able to recognise his father without the use of snapshots. Don't you ever *dare* imply that I tried to trap you! Trap you, indeed,' she sniffed. 'I'd throw you back!'

'You've developed the art of misinterpreting everything I say into a science.' Liam's expression had become more deeply encased in ice with each fresh, brutally frank observation she made. 'I had no idea I was such a failure as a friend. I'm surprised you welcomed me into your home considering my immaturity and promiscuity,' he observed pithily.

'What's perfectly acceptable in a friend can be a bit of an embarrassment in a partner, or father.' If you dish it up, Liam, she decided grimly, be very sure you can take it.

'Damn you, Jo, are you trying to tell me you hate me

that much?' The stark expression of pain in his blue eyes made her own fill with totally unexpected tears.

'But don't you *see*, Liam?' she whispered. 'If you marry me that's exactly how you'll feel about me. You'll grow to resent me—hate me.' If you don't already, she thought miserably. 'I know this thing has blown what we had apart, but if we don't do anything hasty we might just save something. I'd like to do that,' she admitted huskily. 'You must see how unsuitable it would be—look at us now.' She stretched her arms out wide and held her hands palm up. 'Just look at us!' Her arms fell to her sides in a helpless gesture of defeat.

Liam stood in shaken silence for several long moments. 'You're being totally irrational, Jo.'

'I'm pregnant, what's your excuse?' she shot back with a glimmer of humour. 'You're so pigheaded and stubborn I could shake you.' She gave an exasperated sigh.

'You could try,' he agreed equably.

'You don't have to do the *right* thing. There's no social stigma attached to being a single mother these days.'

'Tell that to your ex-bosses at MacGrew and Bartnett, did you?'

'It's their loss.' I really walked right into that one!

'Fighting words, but where do you go from here?'

'I might go freelance, start up on my own.'

'And how much research have you invested in that idea?'

'Lots!' she lied glibly.

She wouldn't give him the satisfaction of admitting the need to wipe that cynical *knowing* look off his face had been the inspiration for the idea. It wasn't as if it was a bad idea; in fact, the more she thought about it...

'You pulled that one out of thin air.'

Jo glared at him and wished she'd had the good sense

to shut the door in his face. 'I'm feeling inspired.' She was also feeling acutely nauseous which did sort of dull her needle-sharp responses. Why, she wondered, do they call it morning sickness? It was the evenings for her—it played havoc with a girl's social life.

'You know you can't have a baby in this flat, don't you?'

Finger on chin, she pretended to cast her mind back. 'No, it was definitely pets, not children in the lease.'

'Be sensible, Jo.'

Fat chance I've got to be anything else, she wanted to shout at him. She knew from experience that thinking about throwing up would undoubtedly anticipate the event.

'This flat is on the third floor, there's no lift, no garden, no space. Have you any idea how much space a baby needs?

'Don't let me interrupt you, you're obviously the expert. Only you'll have to carry on without me.' Hand over her mouth, she fled to the bathroom.

'Running away isn't going to solve anything,' Liam yelled impatiently as he followed her. He was about to push open the door which had swung in his face when the sound coming from inside the room stopped him.

The significance of the noises emanating from within hit him and he rubbed his hand stiffly across his forehead, almost expecting to find the words insensitive and unfeeling tattooed there.

Fifteen minutes later Jo was sitting cross-legged on the bathroom floor feeling she had more in common with a wet dishcloth than a human being. A pair of gleaming black boots came into view, but she didn't look up.

'Can I do anything?'

'Besides lecture me on child-rearing?'

'I was out of order.'

'I thought you'd be out of here by now.' Under the circumstances she felt she was quite restrained in giving him his marching orders so politely.

'I didn't want to barge in earlier,' he said gruffly. 'Can I get you anything?'

'Privacy,' she said bluntly. You had to be blunt with some people.

'Just yell if you want anything. I'm not going anywhere. Sure I can't do anything?' Helplessness was not an emotion Liam was used to and his frustration was clearly visible as he hovered indecisively over her.

'My brow's not fevered and it doesn't need mopping,' she snapped crankily. Even being blunt didn't work with him! Poor Liam. She felt a sudden inconvenient surge of remorse. 'I'm sorry, Liam, but I'm not the grin-and-bear-it type; if you stay around I'm more likely to bite your head off.' She finally looked up, and underneath the exhaustion a faint smile of apology lingered.

She looked worryingly white, her freckles standing out starkly and her copper hair darkened with sweat.

'I'll take the chance.' When the words came they were hoarse. The peculiar strained quality in his tone made Jo look sharply at him.

No wonder he's staring, she thought. I must really look a fright. She wasn't sure her present condition, unpleasant as it was, warranted that sort of expression on his face. He looked—well, shell-shocked was the closest she could come up with. I suppose the realities of pregnancy aren't always that pretty, she reflected. Not when you get up close.

'If past experience is anything to go by I'll be here quite a while yet and all I'll want to do is crawl into bed. If you want to lecture me it'll have to wait until the morning,'

she warned him, just in case he was hanging on in the
hope of making her see the light.

When she made her way some time later to the bedroom
Liam was slumped on her sofa. 'I'm off to bed, you can
let yourself out.'

'How are you feeling?'

'Fine, really.' She was tired and a bit shivery. She'd
shed her clothes in the bathroom and pulled on a fluffy
towelling robe which she hugged around herself now.

'I thought you didn't go in for brave smiles?'

She shot him a wry smile. 'You caught me, it's a female
thing you wouldn't understand. Every man I know makes
a major production out of a cold.' That was one general-
isation she was prepared to defend.

The pristine white sheets on her bed had been neatly
turned down and a jug of iced water stood on the bedside
table. Liam appeared in the doorway. 'Thanks.' The sheets
had been white when she'd shared—stupid! All her sheets
were white. Don't start thinking about *that* now!

'Can I get you tea or anything?'

He was far too big to hover, and her bedroom wasn't
that big to begin with. 'Tea's a major no-no at the moment,' she told him with a shudder. 'Water's fine.'

She opened a drawer and pulled out a fresh nightdress.
It was a nostalgic white lawn affair, ankle-length. She
shook it out. 'Do you mind?' She paused, hand on the tie
of her robe, and gave him a pointed look.

'You obviously do.' He made a meal of turning his back
on her. 'I'll close my eyes if that will help?'

His sarcasm really riled her. So, he's seen it all before,
she thought angrily. It doesn't mean he's got a lifetime's
viewing rights. 'It would help if you just went away.' She
let the robe fall to the floor and wriggled swiftly into the
nightdress.

'I've no intention of leaving until you're safely in bed.'
There was a grim note of finality in his voice.

Safe! Last time he'd been here bed hadn't been at all
safe. This private reflection brought a little colour back
into her pale cheeks.

'You done?'

She nodded and then remembered he couldn't see her.
'Uh-huh.' She picked up her robe and hung it on the hook
on the wardrobe door. Like most of the items in her flat it
was an old, second-hand piece which she'd bought and
imaginatively renovated. She'd rubbed the layers of heavy
dark varnish off it and the wood grain now gleamed
through the misty-blue colour wash. The tedious hours
spent on it had been worth it.

When she turned around he was watching her. Despite
the pin-tucks and modest neckline, in certain lights the
nightgown was transparent. The lighting in the room pro-
vided perfect conditions for this to happen at that moment.

His lips were parted slightly and his eyes half closed as
she frowned enquiringly at him. The brooding expression
on his dark face grew more intense and she saw the muscles in his throat silently work.

'I used to wonder what you looked like, you know, without anything on.' His husky words flowed over her like
the finest silk, insidiously clinging, creating soft flurries of
sensation as it brushed against her skin. 'Did you wonder
what I...?'

Tearing herself from the mesmeric quality of his eyes,
Jo looked down and gave a startled gasp. Even from her
disadvantaged viewpoint she could see the provocative
thrust of her nipples poking through the fabric and the
shadow at the apex of her slim legs against which the soft,
floating fabric clung. Did he think she'd done this on pur-
pose?

'Never!' she squeaked, diving under the covers. 'I've never... Well, only in passing, like you do.' Honesty had a place, she thought with exasperation, but this wasn't it! No matter how platonic a friendship was, curiosity was natural, wasn't it? His body wasn't a subject she thought it wise to linger over too long at the moment.

Liam nodded as though he understood what she was saying completely. Maybe a bit too completely, she thought suspiciously, observing the worrying gleam in his Irish eyes.

'Comfy?' he asked solicitously.

When had he wondered what her body was like? Surely she would have detected any thoughts like that? Now there was no longer a mystery she couldn't help wondering what he thought. Was the reality disappointing?

She couldn't help herself mentally comparing her figure to the numerous girlfriends he'd had over the years. He wasn't fixated on a particular type, you had to give Liam that—he didn't discriminate between blondes, brunettes, tall, petite, voluptuous and athletic. She couldn't remember him ever going out with a redhead, though.

'Fine, thanks.' She really had to stop thinking about him like this!

'I don't know how in that bed,' Liam observed, placing his hand on the foot of the bed and lightly rattling the wooden frame. 'It's not big enough for a pygmy.'

An image of their hot, sweat-drenched bodies entwined on the narrow mattress irresistibly popped into her head. 'It suits me.' Had he wanted to provoke that very image? Or had it been her mind reading too much into a casual observation? Why was she even wondering?

'I'm amazed Justin didn't persuade you to buy something more...spacious.'

'Justin didn't sleep over.' She was too flustered by the

way his eyes skimmed over her face and lower to dissemble.

'But I thought you two...?'

'We did!' she assured him, her face ablaze with embarrassment. There had been a time when she'd been able to discuss anything with Liam without suffering a scrap of self-consciousness. She somehow doubted that time would ever return. 'I always needed to get up early in the morning and... We both like our privacy...'

'God knows what you ever saw in him.' Liam's scornful comment cut into her rambling justification for the lack of passion in her sex life.

Before she hadn't even noticed that the routine of her professional life was echoed in the more private aspects of her life. *Before* she hadn't been aware of a sense of dissatisfaction. Her life seemed to have fallen into two definite areas: life before she'd taken Liam into her bed, and life after. She *must* stop making comparisons.

It felt extremely disloyal to Justin to constantly contrast his lovemaking with the madness of that night. Her state of mind had obviously had a lot to do with it, she told herself—even if they wanted to they couldn't repeat that sort of wild intensity again. Now why did she go and think that?

'I saw a kind, considerate—' she began fiercely.

'Unimaginative, boring...'

'I don't know why you're so mean about Justin—after all, it was you who encouraged me to sleep with him!' she pointed out crossly.

'I did *what*?' In other circumstances the rigid outrage on his face might have made her laugh.

'You were always teasing me about being a...you know—'

'Virgin?'

'Exactly.' She frowned at the interruption, implying with a disdainful glance that she hadn't been struggling for words at all. 'It was you who said I shouldn't wait for some white knight, I should get out there and—'

'I didn't!' he began, his colour heightened.

'Yes, you did. I just followed your advice.'

'For God's sake,' he protested, 'I didn't mean for you to sleep with just anyone, just for the sake of it. It's worth waiting for someone special...' He looked totally appalled at the notion that his joking remarks could have been so influential.

'Like you did,' she put in with sweet-faced malice. He had the grace to look sheepish.

'That's different!'

'It certainly is,' she agreed wholeheartedly. 'What I had with Justin involved neither selfishness or shallow thrill-seeking. For goodness' sake, Liam, don't look so devastated. I didn't jump into bed with Justin just because I thought you felt I ought to, or because you were my role model. I fell in love with him.' Hearing the defiance in her tone made her frown. The admission didn't appear to appease Liam either.

'Then why the hell didn't you want *his* babies? According to you, you've got this biological time bomb ticking away.'

She blinked. Good question. 'Who said I didn't?' she prevaricated glibly.

'You refused to marry him so it logically follows—'

'Oh, don't start flinging your own peculiar brand of logic at me. The timing was wrong, that's all.'

'And now?'

'You can't turn back the clock.'

'If you could...?'

He didn't ask easy questions, did he? 'I wish you'd just

leave me in peace to sleep. I can't think straight, let alone play your stupid games of if onlys.' The dark circles under her eyes gave added weight to this claim; they made Liam back off, anyway.

'Goodnight, Jo.'

She pulled the covers over her head and huddled down. Pity he wasn't always so sensitive to her needs. This thought led irresistibly to a series of sizzling memories that proved beyond any shadow of a doubt just how sensitive Liam *could* be to her needs. He'd seemed to know what she wanted before she did.

The sound of the telephone dragged Jo from a shallow, dream-filled slumber. A light shone from the open door of the living room. She opened her eyes in time to see Liam fling himself at the shrill instrument and grab it off the receiver mid-shriek.

'I'll take it.' She reached out as he picked it up.

He blinked and rubbed his tousled hair when he saw her open eyes. 'Sorry, I tried to get here before it woke you.' The buttons on his shirt had come adrift almost to his waist and his olive-toned skin gleamed in the subdued light. She tore her eyes firmly away from the spectacle of his heavily muscled torso.

'Hello. Hello, Uncle Pat. Yes, yes, he is here.' She grimaced as she passed the phone to Liam. 'It's for you.'

'Father.' His jaw tightened as he listened to the blistering diatribe from the other end. 'There never has been a secret affair.'

Jo glanced at the clock—two-thirty. She could see how Liam being in her flat at that time in the morning might lead his father to believe he'd been lied to. There were some very natural conclusions most people would jump to. Ironically Liam had slept on her sofa several times before—on those occasions they might just have talked too late into the night for it to be sensible for him to go home, or they might have shared a bit too much wine. Nobody had rung on those innocent occasions and it would never have occurred to her to have been embarrassed about the fact he'd slept over.

As she watched Liam listening it soon became obvious that something was wrong—badly wrong. She could see it in the tension that stiffened his big body in a tense, unnatural posture. He rubbed the palm of his hand against the rigid, dark-shadowed line of his angular jaw. The curling sweep of his dark eyelashes was the only hint of softness in his otherwise rather harsh features; right now they cloaked his expression. The strong premonition of disaster settled like an icy stone in the pit of her belly.

'Yes, I understand. I'll be there.'

'What's wrong, Liam?' she asked, anxiety shining in the smoky green depths of her eyes.

The disturbing blankness drained from his eyes as he looked at her. 'It's Mum, they think she's had a heart attack.'

Jo caught her breath sharply. 'She's not…?' She wasn't even aware of raising herself on her knees and grabbing the fabric of his loosened shirt.

'No, she's alive,' he replied immediately. 'They've taken her to The Royal. I'll ring you when I know what's happening.'

'Don't be stupid,' she said, scrambling out of bed. 'I'm coming with you.'

'You can't—'

'I can and I am.' She grabbed underwear from a drawer and tugged the nightdress over her head. The situation put false modesty firmly in its place. It put a lot of things in perspective. Aunt Maggie was one of the dearest people in the world and since her own mother's death she had occupied a very special place in Jo's heart.

Her hurried movements had an innate grace and her total lack of self-consciousness contrasted starkly with her previous awkward posture in his presence. Liam stood for a moment looking at the vulnerable, desirable image of her naked back. The feminine dip of her narrow waist and the gentle flair of hips that bordered on the boyish.

He nodded. 'Fine.'

'I won't be a minute,' she yelled after him. 'Don't go without me.'

'How is she?'

Patrick Rafferty seemed shrunk somehow to Jo's eyes; his big body lacked the vitality she'd always associated with him. He was sitting hunched up in the corner of the small, antiseptic white ante-room into which they'd been directed. He looked up as Liam spoke and Jo was shocked by the anger in his face.

'And you care, I suppose?'

'You know I do.' Liam spoke quietly.

'She's not stopped fretting about you since she learnt about the baby. If you hadn't acted like an irresponsible, selfish adolescent this wouldn't have happened. A bullet would have been kinder,' he accused wildly. 'It was the first thing on her mind every morning she woke up and every night it was the last thing she talked about. It's your fault. The very sight of you makes me sick.' His accent had regressed to the brogue of his youth and his deep voice shook with passion. He got to his feet stiffly; his full height was almost that of his son's. His big hands curled ominously into fists at his side.

Liam didn't offer any excuses or a defence of any kind.

The detached calm she'd watched grow during the journey here seemed to deepen.

'Well!' Liam flinched as his father's deep voice cracked. 'Aren't you going to say anything?'

'Have you seen her, Dad?'

Pat Rafferty dropped back down into his seat and buried his face in his hands. 'The doctors are with her,' he said in a muffled voice.

Jo walked over and took Liam's stiff, cold fingers in her small hand. 'He needs to blame someone,' she said softly.

Liam looked down at their joined hands and then at Jo's face. 'I know.'

'He doesn't mean it.' Her thumb moved in circular motions over his palm. She didn't think she could bear the bleakness in his eyes.

'Of course he means it and why shouldn't he? It's true.' The self-contempt in his voice was like a lash as it struck out. The impotence of her situation made Jo want to cry out. Far better to feel the pain herself than watch someone she loved suffering. And she loved Liam—always had. She couldn't change that any more than she could alter the colour of her eyes.

'Self-pity isn't going to help Aunt Maggie.' She dampened her first instinct which ran vaguely along the lines of throwing herself into his arms. The last thing he needs is me going all cloying and tearful, she decided.

'Go and help Dad, Jo.'

I want to help you, she wanted to cry. The rejection nearly cracked her fragile composure. Just as well she didn't take the emotional option. 'He needs you, Liam.'

Whatever divisions the revelations of his prospective fatherhood had brought about, this tragedy threatened to widen the gulf between father and son. She couldn't take responsibility for that and she couldn't watch that gulf become unbridgeable.

'I don't think so.'

'Well, I know so, *please*, Liam.' He met her pleading glance with all the appearance of disinterest. Jo wasn't fooled—she knew how much he was hurting; she knew the coldness was a façade. She knew how much his father's rejection had hurt him. 'Are you so afraid of the possibility he'll turn his back on you?' She had to taunt just to get through to him.

'I'm not...!' he began, turning on her furiously.

'Swallow your stiff-necked pride, Liam. Don't let your guilt come between you and your father.'

A slow, reluctant smile entered his eyes. 'You always were an interfering little minx.'

'Go on,' she said, giving him a little push, 'what's the odd bloody nose between family?'

It didn't come to that. She watched Liam sit beside his father and begin to speak, his voice low. He hadn't spoken for long when she saw the older man's shoulders begin to heave.

Arms around his weeping father, Liam cast a look of deep gratitude in Jo's direction.

It hit her then. It didn't really shock her as much as it might have—perhaps she'd secretly known all along. Perhaps that was why she hadn't been in any hurry to find a man of her own. Perhaps that was why she had instinctively recoiled at the idea of formalising her tepid romance with Justin. There was no perhaps about the emotion that engulfed her now. She didn't just love Liam, she was *in* love with him.

CHAPTER FOUR

'IT COULD have been worse.' Jo winced as the platitude slipped so readily from her lips.

This need to fill the silence was a new thing. In the past they hadn't needed words to fill comfortable silences—but then this silence wasn't comfortable. It was tense and awkward. Every time Jo looked at Liam she was afraid he would read her thoughts. I don't want his pity, she thought defiantly—he shan't know.

Liam just nodded. 'Are they the day shift?' he wondered out loud as they drove in the opposite direction to the steady stream of traffic entering the hospital. He glanced at his wrist-watch. 'I'd lost track of time,' he observed. 'I suppose I should feed you.'

'I'm easy.'

His lips twitched and the faint flicker of movement became a proper grin. 'No, you're hard work most of the time, but usually worth it.'

She didn't read too much into this comment. It was relief, a manifestation of the euphoria that had been obvious in him since he'd spoken to the doctors.

'You can just drop me off at Dad's.' She hoped he was still in bed. He'd probably go ballistic if he saw her getting out of Liam's car. She wanted the chance to explain about Aunt Maggie before he waded in demanding blood.

'Dare I take the risk? He might have his shotgun handy.' Liam's thoughts were obviously running along similar lines to her own. 'Come to our place, Jo, and I'll cook you something. I need to drop in there. I promised Dad I'd take him in a change of clothes and shaving gear.'

'He needs a rest; you both do.' She shot a swift, covetous look at his profile. He looked as though he hadn't slept in days.

'He won't leave her.'

'No,' she agreed quietly. 'I am quite hungry,' she admitted lightly.

'I'm not surprised after last night,' he observed, referring with a grimace to her sickness.

'It shouldn't last much longer—so they tell me.' She certainly hoped the professionals knew what they were talking about. 'I eat in the morning to compensate for later on. It won't harm the baby,' she reassured him. 'I asked.'

'I wasn't thinking about the baby.'

'Oh! I'm tough,' she assured him earnestly.

'As old boots.'

The affection in the swift sideways glance had the power to suspend her heartbeat. Don't do anything stupid like reading anything but friendship into that, she instructed herself sternly.

The four-wheel drive crunched over the gravelled surface of the long, crescent-shaped driveway. Jo looked out at the horses grazing in the lush paddock the driveway bisected. The horses had originally been a hobby which over the years had grown. Pat Rafferty had retired early from his law practice and was a well-respected and successful breeder these days.

The stables were busy, but the house was empty. She knew the absence of his mother hit Liam as he walked into the kitchen; she felt it herself and her heart ached for him. It was the one room that most echoed the warmth and humour of Maggie's personality.

'I suppose your stomach is a bit delicate?' Liam filled the kettle and placed it on the hotplate of the Aga.

'Not in the mornings.' She pulled out a chair beside the large scrubbed table.

'Bacon, egg…sausage?' He reached for two earthenware mugs.

'Everything, I'm greedy.' The memory came flooding back so abruptly she couldn't breathe. She'd asked for everything before and had she received and given just that!

The sound of the mug smashing into a thousand pieces on the floor broke the sudden electric silence. -

'Hell!' he swore softly. 'Where does Mum keep the dustpan?' His blue eyes had darkened several shades and his olive skin seemed to be drawn tighter over the sharp contours of his face.

She immediately recognised that her light-hearted reply had triggered the same response in him. Knowing her sensual fantasy was being shared only increased the heavy, hot languor that had invaded her entire body. Throat dry, heart thudding, she cleared her throat.

'In the cupboard, over there.' Despite her best efforts it was barely more than a husky whisper.

She ached for his touch; for a moment the yearning blanked out every other thought in her head. How had she been so blind to something that had been staring her in the face? Of course she wanted his child, she wanted every part of him. Greedy didn't begin to cover the ferocity of her desire.

'Thanks. Lucky it wasn't the best china.'

'Yes.' The words didn't mean anything, they just covered the gap in normality. Part of her still longed for that normality, but part of her was no longer satisfied with the comfortable security of their deep friendship. She needed more—much more. What an awful, hopeless situation to find herself in.

'That should do it.' He straightened up suddenly and she flushed, as would anybody caught ogling someone's tight, masculine rear.

'Women look too,' she said belligerently, instinctively defending herself from the glitter of his blue eyes. Why, she wondered despairingly, didn't I just keep my mouth shut like a normal person?

'Was I objecting?' he said, holding up his hands. 'Who needs subtlety? I'm an enthusiastic advocate of girl power.'

I just bet you are. 'Are you laughing at me?' It wasn't surprising—he had all the smug confidence of someone who knew he had a beautiful body and sex appeal that went off the scale.

'The fact I'm laughing at all is a miracle. A miracle only you could have brought about, Jo. You really are unique. Thank you.'

The unexpected and genuine warmth was lovely, but she'd have much preferred he thought of her as sexy and seductive rather than some sort of clown—unique or not.

'I'd prefer feeding than thanking,' she pointed out practically.

'Of course you do, sorry.'

Liam's plate was only half empty when he put his own knife and fork aside and, with his chin resting on steepled fingers, watched her demolish her food.

She was aware of his eyes but she willed herself not to react to his amusement. 'You're a good cook,' she admitted with a sigh as she pushed her empty plate to one side.

'I had a good teacher.'

'Thank you,' she accepted the compliment. 'Actually I think I'd have done my own sex a greater service if I'd refused to give you lessons,' she observed tartly. '*Pulling* females isn't the purest motive for learning the culinary art.'

'It was a great incentive though, and it worked.'

'You did mention it at the time,' she recalled sourly.

'I was young,' he excused himself. 'For boys of a certain age "pulling", as you so delicately phrase it, is a fundamental urge.'

'You mean it changes?'

'So young and so cynical.'

'Perhaps I've got reason to be.' As a mood-breaker this was in a class of its own. As she watched, Liam assumed the appearance of a man with the weight of the world on his shoulders.

It was heartbreaking. If he'd loved her, this baby and all it entailed wouldn't have been a burden. It would have been an adventure, one to be shared and cherished.

'I was talking to Dad.'

'I thought you might have been,' she said slowly. She knew Liam well enough to know this part had been coming. 'I don't suppose my name came up, did it?' She eyed him warily. 'I'm surprised you waited this long to share the pearls of your joint wisdom.'

'I thought you might be more...amenable after I'd fed you.'

'Don't bank on it.' A girl didn't need to be psychic to anticipate an industrial-strength dose of moral blackmail heading in her direction.

'Mum can't be upset at the moment, the doctors made that quite clear. Stress could make all the difference between recovery and...'

'I understand that, of course I do.' Did he think she was stupid?

'You don't want to marry me,' he said flatly.

I'd walk across hot coals to get to the altar if you loved me. 'No,' she agreed firmly, 'I don't.' She frowned. She'd expected him to push this option even harder—he had a lot more at stake now.

'Would an engagement be a compromise you could live with?'

'Doesn't the one usually lead to the other?'

'Not in this case. Hear me out, Jo,' he pleaded urgently, reading the rejection on her face. 'It'll be a cosmetic exercise. Mum will be happy.'

'I can see that it would solve the short-term problem, but what about later on?'

'She'll be stronger then.'

'You've got it all worked out.' She glared at him resentfully. Of course she was going to agree; how could she not? Liam knew she'd do anything for Maggie.

'Desperate circumstances call for desperate action.' There was something scarily uncompromising about his expression.

'Uncle Pat is in on this, then?' She felt trapped. She knew lies had a way of spiralling out of control.

Liam nodded slowly. 'His main priority is getting Mum better. If you can think of another way around this, Jo, I'm all ears.'

It wasn't his ears she had a problem with, although they were rather nice; it was his legs, his washboard-flat stomach and wide, well-muscled chest. Just thinking about the curve of his strong back made her stomach go into spasm. She was even fond of that beaky nose. Once she reached his face she couldn't actually decide which was more disturbing: his glorious eyes or that sinfully sexy mouth.

'That's generous of you. You know I've got to say yes, don't you?' The distress in her voice made his jaw set.

'Do you expect me to lie to my dad too? Can you imagine how hurt he'll be when he finds out?'

'That's up to you, but the fewer people who know the truth, the better. Uncle Bill isn't the world's best actor.'

'Only you could make honesty sound like a defect! I don't know how you can sound so casual about all this!' she accused hotly. 'Aunt Maggie is bound to start making wedding plans—you do realise that, don't you?'

'Can you think of any better therapy for her? Invitations, flowers...'

'That's all well and good,' she hissed in frustration, 'but we're not going to get married.'

'Rome was probably built in a shorter time than it takes for most weddings to be arranged.'

'I think you're thinking of Rome burning.'

'Weddings can be cancelled,' he reminded her. 'You never know, you might decide you want to go through with it after all.'

This offhand remark made her stare at him. The innocent expression in his dark blue eyes only intensified her suspicion. 'I thought you'd accepted that isn't possible.'

'Did I say that?' The hard, determined gleam that entered his eyes made her shiver. 'You're carrying my child, Jo,' he said quietly, his eyes reflexly dropping to her lap. 'I should be the one bringing him up, that's an inescapable fact. I've every intention of making you see that's the right thing to do. I'm confident you'll see sense in the end.'

In the face of such unrelenting determination she felt helpless. 'You've got tunnel vision, Liam Rafferty!' she accused. 'You're even prepared to use Aunt Maggie's...' She stopped, seeing the sudden searing outrage on his expressive face. 'Hell, I don't know why I said that.' She inched her chair forward, scraping it on the tiled floor until she could grasp his arm. She could feel the tension in the corded strength of his forearms.

'I know you wouldn't do that, but you've got to admit you've never been averse to manipulating situations to your advantage,' she excused her response gruffly. 'I just feel...feel things are out of my control.'

She loved him, she couldn't control that, but she wasn't going to enter into a marriage of convenience under any circumstances.

'I don't understand why you're so anti the idea of marrying me.'

'Shall I list the reasons in alphabetical order?'

'I'm not exactly a stranger,' he pointed out reasonably.

'Neither is Jim the postman, but I'd say no to him too.'

'I should hope so—he's got a wife and four kids.'

'This isn't a laughing matter.'

'I'm not laughing, Jo, I'm banging my head against a brick wall. We've got plenty in common, I make you laugh, we're compatible in bed...'

'That...that's...' Her scornful laugh emerged as a croak.

'True,' he finished bluntly. 'Why does it bother you so much?'

'It doesn't bother me.' She affected a careless shrug. 'That night was a mistake, a one-off. If I hadn't been feeling so emotional and—there were...call it a freak set of circumstances.'

'Then why do I keep catching you looking at me like I'm the dessert trolley? You're famous for your sweet tooth, Jo.'

One elbow on the table, he rested his chin in his hand and waited for her response with a disturbing smile that was half taunt, half challenge. She was desperately aware that he was watching her from under the sweep of those ridiculously long eyelashes. Determined she wasn't going to compound her transparent behaviour any farther, she consciously wiped her face clean of emotions.

'And you're famous for your over-inflated ego!' If one could die of sheer humiliation she'd be stretched out on the floor right now. That must have been a stab in the dark, she decided hopefully. There's no way I've been *that* obvious?

'There's one simple way of proving who's right.'

He didn't mean…! Yes, that was *exactly* what he meant. 'You always did want the last word, but that's ludicrous. You don't *really* think I'm going to melt into some compliant, gibbering heap if you touch me, do you?'

'*You* obviously think so,' he said, watching the agitated movements of her breasts under the fluffy angora sweater she wore with deep interest. 'Pregnancy has made some very flattering changes in your body over the past few weeks.'

The tension in her rigid shoulders felt like red-hot needles as her muscles screeched in protest. Panic clawed in the pit of her stomach. She couldn't let him touch her; even if she didn't blurt out the truth he'd be bound to guess.

'If you lay one finger on me this deal is off, Liam, I'm not joking.' She licked her dry lips.

Liam took in her wide, dilated eyes and shallow, swift respirations. A fierce frown formed on his face. 'What the hell are you scared of? Me?' He sounded shocked and outraged at the notion. 'Anyone would think I was about to rape you!'

'I'm just laying down a few ground rules.' She realised with dismay that she had failed miserably to take the dangerous intensity out of the situation.

'Ground rules—hell!' he swore savagely. 'Do you think I'd force you to do anything?' His nostrils flared with disgust. 'If I was picking up the wrong signals all you had to do was tell me.'

'Don't overreact, Liam.'

'Me?'

'This thing is complicated enough without adding a more…more…'

'Intimate element.'

'Exactly.'

'Then the idea of being intimate with me leaves you cold?'

'Not cold, exactly,' she confessed, her glance sliding away from his sharp eyes.

'Then *what* exactly?'

'I'm pregnant!' Liam and his damned persistence. Why couldn't he leave well alone?

'That hadn't slipped my mind.'

Only in his dreams, she thought bitterly. Deep down he had to resent this situation which had been thrust upon him.

'Are you planning nine months of celibacy?' He seemed to find the notion amusing, she discovered resentfully as she watched him tilt his chair back to a dangerous angle.

Probably a lot more. 'Lively redhead, good sense of humour, looking for warm, sensitive man. Incidentally I'm pregnant.' The sugary smile faded dramatically from her face and her voice hardened. 'This is the real world, Liam. How many replies do you think I'll get to that one?'

'You'd probably be surprised. A lot of men are attracted by the whole fertility thing.'

'You mean the personal columns are read by a lot of weirdos.'

'A lot of lonely people, I should think. I'm certainly not repelled by the idea of pregnancy—where does that put me on your weirdo scale?'

'That's different.' She eyed him doubtfully. Did he expect her to believe he'd find her attractive when her waist was a dim and distant memory? He *sounded* sincere, though. His words did provide her with a startling and unexpected insight which intrigued and, if she was totally honest, even excited her.

'That's true, I'm your baby's father—a fact you find more convenient to forget.'

'Don't do me any favours, Liam. Your job finished three months ago.'

'The way I recall it it was a pleasure.' His heavy eyelids drooped over his half-closed eyes. 'You're thinking about it now.' His voice had dropped to a low, suggestive drawl that brushed against her sensitised nerve-endings. 'I can see it in your face. Don't shake your head, Jo, it's true. Tell me, does that blush go all over? I'd really like to find out.'

'You can't say things like that to me,' she replied in a tone tinged with desperation. She silently cursed her fair redhead's skin, which was always a clear barometer of her feelings.

'I'm not following some script here, Jo, I'm just saying what comes naturally.'

'It's not…not appropriate.' His hoot of laughter made her full lips compress into a straight line of disapproval. 'As for you being spontaneous—don't make me laugh! Everything you're doing is designed specifically to push me into a corner—to make me do what *you've* decided is best for me.'

'There is no me and you, just us,' he said simply.

'I can't argue with you when you're like this,' she said, her eyes searching his determined face. 'You're impossible!'

'But kind of cute.'

She closed her eyes. If cute was all he was she might have stood a chance, but Liam was that and a whole lot more, and she loved all of it, even the stubborn, impossible part. How had she ever missed the fact he was the most *male* man she'd ever encountered? He gave a whole new meaning to virility. He was, quite simply, irresistible.

'Do you really find pregnant women attractive?' Her curiosity couldn't be silenced.

'You make it sound like some sort of perversion.' He laughed at her self-conscious expression. 'I don't know why you're so surprised—child-bearing is the one true female mystery, and men are naturally intrigued by something so essentially female. Forget girl power, it's *woman* power, and a man will always prefer a woman to a girl. There's something...I don't know, earthy, sensual, about motherhood.'

Deep down her body shuddered in a helpless response to his provocative words. The ripples tracked through her body like fingers of molten fire. 'Are you saying a woman has to bear children to prove her femininity?'

'I wouldn't have thought any two are alike, but then I wouldn't know, Jo, I'm not a woman.'

'I'd noticed.'

'I've noticed you noticing. Jo?'

The question, invitation, in his voice made her want to throw caution and self-respect to the winds. Paralysis was beginning to take hold in the tingling extremities of her body. To be seduced by the gravelly suggestion in his deep voice or the still, explosive quality in his body was insanity. She had to do something drastic to snap this spell before things went mad again.

'Shall I help you pack some things for Maggie?'

'Fine, if that's the way you want it.' His cheek-bones still seemed sharp and prominent in his angular face. The outline of his sensually sculpted lips seemed oddly exaggerated. She could identify readily with the seething frustration in his eyes.

It isn't me he wants, she reminded herself, it's the mother of his child he wants to bind more firmly to his side.

'What are we going to tell your mum when we eventually call things off?' She followed his example and got to her feet. 'Or haven't you thought that far ahead?'

'We could say that the idea of me touching you is distasteful. That we're physically incompatible.' He came behind her and pulled the chair away as she straightened up.

She found his humour rather cruel—deliberately so, she suspected. 'I don't think that will be suitable.' The fact he was standing so close had her quivering like one of the young horses in the exercise yard.

'Or true.' He bent forward and she felt his warm breath touch her cheek.

She twirled around and found her face on a level with his chest. 'You slept with me out of pity and now we're having a child. I'm not about to make that mistake worse by marrying you, no matter how much I want...' She stopped, appalled at what she'd almost said...want to touch you, taste you, feel you as part of me!

'We wouldn't have to worry about you getting pregnant.'

Her shocked eyes collided with his smouldering blue ones. 'You misunderstood...' she began shakily. A girl tended to get a bit shaky when a man looked at her with such raw *need*.

He shook his head. 'Talking about misunderstandings,' he said, pushing his fingers throughout the silky strands of her burnished hair. She let out a soft sound as his fingers moved around the back of her neck. 'I didn't sleep with you out of pity, Jo.'

'Perhaps pity is the wrong word.' Her head fell back against his kneading fingers.

'It sure as hell is.' His other hand came up until he cradled her skull, holding her face up towards him.

'You don't have to do this, you know.' It was hard to form a thought, let alone force the words past the emotional constriction in her throat. 'I'm not going to run back to Justin.'

She felt him stiffen. 'You think that's why I'm doing this?'

'Well, aren't you?' With all her heart she wished it weren't so, but she couldn't see any other explanation—unless...? 'I've been so stupid!' She'd been so wrapped up in her own feelings she'd not paused to think about how *he* was feeling. He'd had a traumatic night; his mother had almost died! What could be more natural than to look for comfort from a friend? She wasn't likely to forget he'd done as much for her.

Liam's fingers slid out of her hair and, taking a step backwards, he looked at her almost warily. 'I'm not about to offer any arguments.'

'I remember how I felt when mum died—I wanted to block it out.' Liam's immobility was somehow worrying.

'So you lost yourself by having mindless sex with the first available male,' he stated matter-of-factly.

'I was only a child...'

'But that's what you think I am doing now?' He completely ignored her faltering response as his chest swelled to impressive proportions with outrage.

She was forced to face the distinct possibility that she'd jumped to the wrong conclusion. The barbed edge to his voice made her wince.

'I'm your friend, I want to help. I'd do anything to help,' she assured him sincerely.

'Does that mean your body is on offer?' He turned away but she could see the vein in his temple throbbing. 'Don't bother replying; for some reason self-sacrifice turns me right off. I'm peculiar that way.'

'I wasn't...' she protested.

'No?' he drawled. 'It sure as hell sounded that way from where I'm standing. If you want to rationalise the fact you want me to make love to you—fine! But don't expect me to co-operate.'

Jo's shoulders sagged; that was the last time she tried any amateur analysis. 'I think we got our wires crossed,' she said tentatively.

'Crossed? I think you severed our lines of communication some time ago, Jo. Now do you mind helping me get Mum's things together? I should be getting back to the hospital.'

Miserably aware she'd made a bad situation worse, she followed him out of the room.

'Pat will fly the Canadian family over, of course.'

'All of them?' Maggie Rafferty's spouse, despite his stoical silence up to this point, felt impelled to query.

'Who are you going to leave out, Pat?' his wife enquired, looking up from her list.

He held up his hands admitting defeat. 'Whatever you say, my darling. Just my luck the damned Raffertys breed like rabbits,' he said in laughing aside to his son.

He was a happy man. In his eyes the enthusiasm with which his wife had seized on the news of his son's prospective wedding had fully justified any slight manipulation of the truth.

'Patrick!'

'What have I done now?' He followed the direction of his wife's gaze to Jo's flushed cheeks. 'What?' he said blankly, then his social gaffe suddenly dawned on him and he shuffled his feet like an oversized schoolboy and looked sheepish.

'It's time for my walk,' she said to her husband. 'Doctor's orders,' she explained to Jo. 'Come along before you put your other foot in it,' she added, taking the big man's arm. 'Seize the moment, Liam,' she advised somewhat obscurely as she left the room.

'She's enjoying herself.'

Jo nodded dubiously. The whole thing had escalated to ludicrous, horrible proportions. Always scrupulously, and often painfully, honest, she was finding the whole charade a terrible strain. Extricating herself from a maze of lies, which grew more convoluted by the hour, was going to be a nightmare.

'This is all costing so much money. I hate cheating. I feel constantly guilty.'

'It's kinder to lie sometimes.' Liam airily brushed aside her doubts.

'What are you doing?' she asked as he very obviously peered behind the heavy folds of the damask curtain which framed the elegant floor-length windows.

'I'm just checking for surveillance equipment.'

'Have you finally flipped?'

'Mum has been so anxious to guide my faltering steps in the right direction that I wouldn't put anything past her.'

'What direction?'

'This direction.'

Jo stared. The box wasn't new, but it wasn't the aged purple velvet that had her attention. The single emerald was square cut; it was breathtaking.

'It's beautiful,' she breathed.

Liam looked pleased by her reaction. 'Mum's grand-mother gave it to her, but it goes farther back than that. It was a man's signet ring originally, but some romantically inclined ancestor of mine had it cut down to size for his lady love. It should fit you.' His narrowed eyes mentally assessed the slender width of her long, tapering fingers tipped by a shiny coral varnish.

Jo caught her breath and glanced up at him in alarm. 'No!' she said, making vague fluttery gestures of rejection with her trembling hands. 'I can't wear that.'

'If it doesn't fit I can—'

'I'm not talking about fit.'

'Then what...?'

'It's too valuable.'

'It's insured. Mum wants you to wear it.'

'That makes it worse,' she wailed in agitation.

'Nonsense!' he said with bracing insensitivity. 'In Mum's world, when a girl gets engaged she wears a ring. In not immediately providing you with one I've committed a social solecism of world-class proportions. This is a prop, nothing more.' He caught hold of her hand and firmly slid the heavy gold band onto her finger. 'There, it fits like a glove.'

'More like a manacle,' Jo retorted as she struggled to pull the slim band off. 'It's stuck!'

'As always, your enthusiasm for our engagement bowls me over.' Beneath the arid humour in his tone there was a definite edge of anger. 'For God's sake, calm down, Jo.'

At his sharp words Jo did stop tugging at the ring. Keeping their brittle relationship from evolving into a slanging match was requiring a lot of self-restraint. 'It's so symbolic,' she said with a small shudder.

A look of raw pain crossed Liam's face before he said

harshly, 'That's the general idea: symbolic of commitment.'

'Symbolic of a lie.'

'Is this a lie?'

His action was so unexpected that she froze in shock. She was unable to tear her eyes away from the sight of his long fingers curling possessively over the lower part of her abdomen. The slight filling out of the flat contours of her belly was all but invisible still when covered by her clothes. Gentle but fiercely possessive, his fingers splayed out as a rapt expression spread over his face.

'This is amazing,' he gasped hoarsely.

'I know.' She'd ached to share it with him; the poignancy of the moment threatened to overwhelm her.

'I want to share this, Jo. Please let me?'

He couldn't know what he was asking. Take him on his terms: marriage to give their child a real family? She could do it, but at what cost to herself? Liam didn't love her and every day together would remind her of that. Oh, he'd be such a great dad! Could she deprive her unborn child of that opportunity? The fierce internal struggle brought beads of perspiration to her upper lip.

'Don't shut me out, Jo, and I don't just mean from the baby. I want to see all the changes in your body as it ripens.' His free hand went to the curve of her breast. Under his light touch her nipples instantly hardened and swelled. A slow smile of sensual satisfaction curved his lips. 'Don't go back to your place tonight; stay with me. Let me look after you.'

'That sounds very paternal.'

'I don't feel paternal.' His grin was devilish. 'At least not towards you.'

'Just the big brother I never had.'

He winced. 'Did I ever say that?'

'Frequently, in your more condescending period.' The hungry response of her body to his touch made a mockery of the last two weeks of self-denial.

His hand travelled up from the upper slope of her breasts to curve around her neck. He pulled her head closer and covered her mouth without any preliminaries. Her soft lips parted under his and at the sound of her deep moan the hungry ferocity of his mouth increased.

When he lifted his head she felt dizzy, almost as if she were floating. Liam's expression was taut and unfamiliar; a dark flush showed along his cheek-bones.

'Come home with me.'

'Are you asking me to live with you?'

'Give it a try, Jo. Call it a trial marriage.'

'Call it crazy.' She didn't want to talk, she didn't want to think! She wanted his mouth on hers, his hands on her body with a desperation that precluded sane consideration.

'That's settled, then.' A fierce light of satisfaction gleamed in his eyes.

'It is?'

The he was kissing her again and she'd have agreed to just about anything to have him go on. Liam heard the door open before she did and he drew back. Her fingers were still tangled in his dark hair when she heard Aunt Maggie speak.

'She liked the ring, then,' Maggie observed, rubbing her hands in delight.

'Maggie, perhaps we should take another turn around the block,' Pat suggested as he tactfully averted his eyes from the young couple.

'Nonsense, Jo and I have a lot more to discuss. Liam can have her any time.'

And wasn't that the truth? Jo thought bleakly.

CHAPTER FIVE

'SO HERE we are.' Jo's bright and breezy tone lacked conviction.

She'd always felt completely at ease here in Liam's home and this abrupt transition to self-conscious edginess was hard to come to terms with. She walked over to the far wall which was almost completely glazed. She looked out blindly towards the great view of the river. The same view could be enjoyed from his roof garden, which she usually tended while he was travelling. It was a tranquil oasis in the middle of the city.

'Here we are indeed. Sorry about the mess. I didn't think I'd be having a visitor.'

'Didn't you?'

His eyebrows lifted and his smile neither confirmed nor denied her suspicions. 'It's the books, I never seem to have enough space to put them,' he observed with an uncharacteristically vague expression. 'And I never did get around to replacing my cleaning lady.'

Jo wasn't fooled. Whilst his words and manner might be casual, she was aware that the expression in his eyes was anything but that. He was sifting and analysing every nuance in her voice, every flicker on her face. It wasn't very comfortable being under a microscope, especially when she had a secret she didn't intend sharing with anyone—least of all Liam!

Two could play at normality. 'It's a mess on a much grander scale than I'm accustomed to.'

'The idea of moving up in the world doesn't seem to be making you very happy, Jo.'

'Well, I hope you don't expect me to earn my bed and board by picking up your socks. It's not funny,' she added as he laughed. To her relief the laughter seemed to have taken the edge off the intensity she sensed coiled just below the surface.

'The idea of you as a domestic slave is extremely funny,' he contradicted firmly. 'And actually I'm quite self-sufficient in the domestic department. I've just outgrown this place,' he mused thoughtfully.

'Outgrown? My flat is a shoebox compared to this, but then I don't get paid megabucks.' I don't get paid at all at the moment, she remembered with a frown. 'Don't think I'm going to scrounge off you. I'm not broke.' She was always self-sufficient; the idea of being reliant on anyone went against the grain.

'You've taken a weight off my mind.'

His sarcastic tone made her flush. She turned away from the window and placed her hands on the back of a leather chair. 'Have you a problem with that?'

'Me?' His blue eyes opened innocently wide. 'Do you want a rent book?'

'I'm trying to be serious.'

'Then turn your mind seriously to this: we'll need to look for somewhere more suitable before the baby comes. Whereabouts would you like to live?'

Neat, but not very subtle. Jo felt snared by his guileless blue gaze. 'You're very generous with the *we* all of a sudden,' she responded spikily.

'Do I detect a certain ambivalence towards this trial marriage?' Despite the lightness in his tone she could sense the irritation beyond the irony.

'I don't know how you talked me into this,' she muttered mutinously. I must be totally crazy, she decided, wondering why on earth she'd fallen in with his scheme. Live with him—what a recipe for disaster!

'I didn't talk you into it, I *kissed* you into it.'

Jo's slight frame swelled with indignation as she glared wrathfully at him. 'My God, but you're so conceited, Liam!' It was humiliating to know how painfully correct his words were. It was also scary that he recognised her weakness.

'I'm only trying to be accurate.'

She snorted derisively at the innocent expression in his blue eyes and the corner of his mouth lifted into a disturbingly attractive grin.

'You became infinitely more pliable.' To her dismay he didn't let the awkward subject drop. 'In fact the change was astounding,' he continued, his voice soft and silkily suggestive.

Jo averted her face to hide the pink glow that stained her cheeks. She pushed aside a pile of papers and sat down in the deeply upholstered leather swivel chair. 'The kissing wasn't personal.'

Liam, elbows on the work counter that separated the kitchen from the living area, rested his chin in his palm and raised an enquiring brow. 'Do tell, I'm fascinated.'

'Fascinated!' she spat in disgust. 'Your trouble is too many women have told you you're *fascinating* and you believe them!' she observed with a sniff. 'The explanation is perfectly simple. I'm being engulfed by hormones and...and...' Pragmatic without being revealing wasn't that easy a balance to achieve. Her aching throat closed over completely.

'You're a raging torrent of primeval want and need—'

She prayed he didn't know just how shockingly perceptive his flippant words were.

'It's easy for you to joke,' she began hotly. Liam had to be the most callous, insensitive male in creation. This was a painfully embarrassing subject and he was playing it for laughs. Probably she ought to act as if the subject were some huge joke too, but she didn't think she could have raised even a feeble grin.

'Who said I was joking?'

Moments before she'd wanted him to show a bit of respect for the gravity of the situation, but now she couldn't detect even the faintest glimmer of a smile in his eyes she wasn't so sure.

'Perhaps joke wasn't quite the right word,' she corrected a little breathlessly. What girl wouldn't be breathless under the impact of Liam's steady, unflinching gaze?

'What is the right word, Jo?'

Jo shook her head to break the mesmeric effect of his blue eyes. 'I only agreed to this to convince Aunt Maggie nothing's fishy.'

'I thought, hormones aside, you didn't know why you agreed.'

'That was a figure of speech.' Trust Liam to be pedantic. '*Mum* has had no trouble accepting the fact we're getting married.'

'I don't have a problem with the idea, because we're *not* getting married.'

He dismissed her protest with an indulgent smile that made her teeth grind. 'In her world,' he continued, 'it's what two people do when they've made a baby.'

In Liam's world too, it seemed. '*Before* they've made the baby is the more conventional process.'

'Is that what Justin had in mind?' As always the thought of Jo's ex-lover soured his mood. He mentally included the *ex* with some satisfaction.

This unexpected inclusion of Justin in the conversation

made Jo blink. Her expression grew belligerent as she watched Liam's lip curl with distaste. 'None of your damn business,' she said stonily.

'He being such a *conventional* sort of guy.'

'And wanting to marry me isn't conventional?'

'No,' he flung back, 'it's an uphill battle!'

Jo regarded his expression of frustrated irritation with sympathy. Guilt combined with some outmoded sense of honour were the only things that had inspired Liam to consider matrimony. 'Some men aren't meant to marry.'

'And you think I'm one of that number?' he asked. Why should he resent her comment? Jo continued to puzzle over the curious expression on his face as he came to sit companionably on the arm of her chair. At least, it might have felt companionable once—now the proximity made her pulse behave in an irregular fashion and her throat grow painfully dry.

'Could be. If you do ever marry I think it will be to someone more decorative and amenable than me.'

'That doesn't restrict the field too much,' he murmured drily as she inclined her head to look up at him.

'I'd never suggest you're too selfish and feckless to marry.' No girl liked to be told she wasn't decorative. Just because she had weakly fallen in with his plans it was no reason to let him get too smug.

'Perish the thought.'

'This is a purely business arrangement.'

'No kissing?'

'Absolutely not,' she agreed without a flicker to show how much havoc the sly question had wrought. It was about time she started showing a bit of self-restraint. She could only blame her hormones just so much! It definitely *wasn't* the right time to dwell on how good Liam's kissing technique was.

'There's something very challenging about rules.'

Jo gave a faint grimace. It was a bit late to remember that as a boy Liam never had been able to resist walking on the forbidden stretch of grass. Even now he had a confrontational attitude to authority if he thought it misplaced.

He moved his hand to the back of her chair and several strands of her hair snagged in the heavy metal strap of his wrist-watch.

Jo cried out sharply as her head was yanked backwards.

Liam instinctively dropped to his knees beside her. 'Keep still!' he ordered tersely, bending forward. His fingers brushed her cheek as he carefully released her. 'Better?' he asked as the pressure on her scalp desisted.

'Uh-huh,' she murmured, running her fingers through her unruly curls. To her dismay Liam didn't straighten up and move away. His body stayed curved over her, one hand steadying himself on the back of the chair, the other a whisper away from her face. The flickering sensation in the pit of her belly became a warm thrumming as the scent of his body made her nostrils flare.

The side of his nose rubbed gently down the side of hers and the barely visible fresh crop of stubble on his jaw grazed against her cheek. His breath came warm against her skin. The intimacy was devastating.

'This isn't actually kissing, is it?' he asked softly.

'Not strictly speaking,' she agreed hoarsely. His eyes were half closed as his fingers moved whisper-like over the firm, rounded contour of her jaw. She suddenly fiercely wanted to press her lips against the lazy droop of his eyelids. Her own fingers still pressed to the side of her head collided with his and, even whilst the tiny gasp was emerging from her lips, his fingers were interlocking firmly with her own.

'This isn't fair!' she groaned as he pulled her hand against his own face.

'What's not fair?'

'I know what you're doing,' she told him hoarsely.

'I always said you weren't as stupid as you look,' he said throatily.

'You think if you get me into bed I'll agree to anything you say.' Jo banged her head against a mental brick wall as these incautious words escaped. She could only hope and pray Liam didn't appreciate the revealing nature of her remark. Trouble was, Liam was too sharp by half to miss much.

'I'm not going to marry you, Liam, and one day you'll thank me for it. Don't do that!' she groaned, closing her eyes tightly. The melting was like a chain reaction she had no control over; it started in the pit of her belly and spread—

'Why?'

'Because I don't like having my ear slobbered over,' she lied wildly. There was nothing even faintly slobber-like about the delicate, agonising things he was doing to her. The fine, downy hairs on her body stood erect as the tingle surged all the way down to her toes.

She opened her eyes to see if this slur had had the desired effect. It swiftly became apparent that his ego had emerged unscathed from this insult. His confident smile was deeply disturbing. As her eyes slid from his face his forefinger on the tip of her chin gently forced her head farther upwards.

'Why are you scared of enjoying yourself?'

'I...I'm not,' she stammered.

'Not enjoying yourself, or not scared?' The warmth in his face almost made it hard to remember why she mustn't let her guard drop.

'Both…neither.'

'Marry me, Jo,' he said, his voice deep with sudden urgency. His fingers moved to cup her face. 'I know it's not what either of us planned, but it makes sense. We could have fun.'

'Fun?' she echoed. She didn't want sense, she wanted glorious, irrational love! She ought to be glad he couldn't see this but his ignorance of her true feelings made her angry and resentful.

'Sure, why not? Haven't we always? You're the only female I know I could contemplate living with and staying sane.'

'Then it's just coincidence you're only proposing now when I'm pregnant. It was your plan all along.' Her lips twisted in a bitter, ironic little smile as she tried to shake her head, but Liam's grip held her immobile. He wouldn't let her look away. It was as if he felt he could convince her of the truth of his claims by the sheer intensity of his conviction.

'You didn't plan to get pregnant, I didn't plan to get married.' His wide shoulders lifted fractionally. 'So what? You are and I can.'

He could, but that didn't mean he wanted to—not deep down. 'You make it sound so simple.'

'It is, Jo.' His eyes drilled into her.

'We'd be getting married for all the wrong reasons.' She could tell from the brief flare of satisfaction in his eyes— and was there some relief there too?—that Liam sensed her struggles were weakening.

'The divorce courts are filled with people who got married for the *right* reasons. We've got a lot going for us.'

'If people in love fail, what chance do we stand?' She felt her eyes fill with tears. The image of his dark, dear familiar face grew misty.

'*In love,*' he repeated derisively. 'What the hell does that mean? You laugh at my jokes, that's a lot more important than some generic term to cover animal attraction. Love has been hyped out of all recognition by popular fiction and teenage girls' magazines. Your old granny couldn't say she was getting married because that was the only way she could respectably have sex—it was much more proper to say she was in love.'

His cynicism shocked her. When had he grown so jaundiced in his outlook? Or had he always been that way and she hadn't noticed?

'I think we should leave my granny out of this, Liam. Say for the sake of argument what you say is true. Why, in an age when virginity is no longer rated so highly, do people still get married?'

'Probably for the same reasons we are, even if they don't realise it. To form a secure family unit. Also it gives both partners an often erroneous belief that they have exclusive rights over their partner.'

She couldn't help but notice that Liam wasn't offering her even an illusion of exclusivity and he wasn't asking for it either.

'I thought you found security boring?' Her words grew blurred as his thumb traced the outline of her full lips.

'I don't find the idea of us sharing a bed boring, any more than you do.'

An incredulous gasp escaped her lips. 'If I do marry you it'll be your touching modesty that swings it.'

The little nip at his thumb was meant to be by the way of playful punishment. Unfortunately it was immediately obvious from the scorching expression in his eyes that Liam didn't recognise the whimsical nature of the assault—the mundane abruptly became erotic. Jo jerked her head back, but the faintly salty taste of his skin lingered on her tongue. Her body throbbed with awareness and she felt the tension in his hard body hike up several notches.

'Let's not waste any more time, Jo.' The coaxing tone of reason had been replaced by something much more authoritative and urgent. 'Most people think we've been sleeping together for years anyway.'

'They don't!' Eyelids that had been succumbing to the heavy warmth that suffused her body flickered open.

'Of course they do.'

For some reason the idea horrified her. 'I don't suppose you did anything to disabuse them...' she began indignantly.

'What do you take me for?' he snarled, his voice harsh with disgust. A light which was almost reckless entered his eyes as he looked down into her pale, delicate features. 'Do you think I'm so desperate to bolster my macho image? Mind you, if I'd known...' His hoarse words trailed suggestively away and Jo saw the muscles in his throat work hard as he swallowed.

'Known what?' she whispered. Her whole body was bathed in an aching tension that heightened all her responses, yet conversely dulled her brain until it was functioning at its most basic level. A level that was concerned with taste and touch and smell; a level filled with shocking appetites and needs.

'How incredible it would be.'

The scornful laugh had metamorphosed into a strangled croak by the time it emerged from her lips. 'So incredible you couldn't wait to forget it had ever happened.' There was bitter accusation in her voice. She couldn't forget that in all the letters they'd exchanged he hadn't referred to that night once! He'd appeared to have wiped out the experience.

'You wanted it that way. Didn't you?'

She shifted uncomfortably under his scrutiny. 'I still do.' She was stubborn in her defiance.

'I might not have mentioned it, but I certainly thought about it.'

His words slid neatly under her crumbling guard. 'Oh!' Any inclination she had to dismiss his words as a useful fabrication died as she searched his face.

'Did *you*?' His blunt question tore away the last shreds of her crumbling composure.

A simple admission would be too revealing. 'I had plenty to remind me,' she reminded him, looking downwards and placing her hand on the slight swell of her belly. When his big hand covered her own she froze. He had beautiful hands, strong and shapely with long, tapering fingers. She looked at the one that covered her own almost greedily.

'You may not be in love with me, Jo, but you love me.' He paused long enough for her to deny it before continuing. 'As I love you.'

'It's not enough.'

'It's a good place to start from.' Her words glanced off his steely determination. 'It's crazy to feel guilty because we're sexually attracted to one another.'

'I'm not guilty!'

'No?' he drawled. 'Then why are you trying to pretend you want me to stop touching you? You don't—'

'Says you.' The scornful put-down came out as a breathy whisper.

'I do say,' he asserted confidently. 'Under the circumstances we should be celebrating the fact we lust after each other. It gives our marriage a much better chance of surviving; sex is important. And later when the lust has faded we'll still be friends.'

'I can hardly wait.' For a bright man he could be extraordinarily stupid sometimes. He'd chosen the one argument that guaranteed her continued lack of co-operation, the one argument that broke her heart. 'I can see I'm going to have to be blunt.'

'Just for a change.'

His sarcastic mutter drew a narrow-eyed glare. 'Why don't you give up, Liam? I'm not marrying you. You're wasting your time. How does that saying go? You can take a horse to water, but you can't make it drink…? The same goes for a girl and the altar.'

'But I can take you to bed and make you agree to anything. I might not be word perfect but I think that was the general gist?'

Jo's eyes widened with dismay. She knew it had been over optimistic to think he'd missed that colossal slip. His expression was one of obstinate confidence as he moved abruptly. She gave a shriek as he swung her up into his arms.

'Put me down this instant!' The angle he held her at made the wild swings of her legs beat uselessly at fresh air. 'Did you hear what I said?' she panted. 'Are you mad?' she demanded, using the ice in her voice to disguise her rising panic. Excitement, no matter how furtive, she chastised herself firmly, had no place in this situation.

'So, I'm in your bed.' It wasn't easy to convey icy disdain when you were struggling inelegantly to sit upright, but she did quite well. 'What does that prove? Other than the obvious fact the evolutionary leap from Neanderthal has passed you by completely. I had no idea your success in the bedroom relied so heavily on beating your conquests into submission.'

Liam was sitting on the edge of the bed facing her. Before he turned his back on her and rested his face in his hands she had a chance to see the dull colour run up under his tan.

'I'd cut off my hand before I'd hurt you, Jo, and well you know it.' As he straightened up he rolled his neck from side to side as if to ease the tension in his well-developed muscles.

His voice, thick with anguished emotion, should have gone straight to her heart, but it went to a much more vulnerable area first—her stomach, where the muscular spasms were like tightening fists. With a cry she scrabbled to her knees on top of the quilt.

'I know that, Liam,' she cried huskily as she wrapped her arms around his neck and rested her head against his back. She hugged hard as regret and love overwhelmed her. What was she doing, punishing him because she loved him? Whatever her motivation each thrust that hit home was inevitably an own goal; she felt his pain as if it were her own.

The warmth of her slim, supple and femininely soft body penetrated through the thin knitted fabric of the shirt Liam wore. The anger and guilt he felt rolled away miraculously as she pressed so close he could feel the heat of her breath as it dampened a small patch of his shirt. As he registered the softness of her breasts pressed against his back she shifted a little to ease the pressure. The tiny gesture reminded him of the changes in her body, changes he had helped bring about.

Abruptly he twisted sideways and his fingers brought her face up to meet his. With his free hand he pulled her across the angle of his hip and onto his lap. He could only feel compliance in her body and nothing she did told him he was reading her body language wrong. She didn't speak at all, just looked at him. Her marvellous green eyes appeared slightly unfocused. He didn't speak either, his vocal cords felt as if an invisible hand had his throat in a stranglehold. A strangle hold almost as strong as the desire that coursed through the rest of his body.

He positioned a pillow under her head as he very carefully laid her back onto the mattress.

Jo's lips felt full and tender. The kiss had been controlled but thorough. She had had plenty of time to appreciate the firm texture of his lips and the flavour of his warm mouth. Time to realise how empty her world would be if she never felt his kiss again.

'I can't think of any reason in the world we shouldn't do this.' The distinctive gravelly edge of his deep voice was more pronounced than she'd ever heard it.

His hands rested either side of her face as, straightarmed, his upper body curved over her. I love you, she reflected, would have been a pretty drastic reply.

'Things will just get more convoluted and complicated,' she warned him huskily. Inside she wanted him to ignore her warning, she *prayed* for him to ignore her warning. If his expression was anything to go by she was pretty confident he would do exactly that.

'Not if we're upfront and honest with each other. This isn't happening just because I want to persuade you to marry me, if that's what you're bothered about.'

'Isn't it?' She couldn't resist touching, ever so softly, the tensed sinews of his forearms. A tiny guttural sound of pleasure escaped her lips before she guiltily withdrew her hand.

'No,' he replied firmly. 'But that's not to say I won't use it to corroborate my case.'

His scrupulous honesty made her smile weakly. She was feeling weak—weak and needy.

'Why is this happening, then, Liam?' she asked languidly.

'This is happening, Jo, because we want it to. My God.' His voice cracked and an expression close to incredulity crossed his contorted features. 'I don't just want, Jo...!' His chest lifted as he gulped to fill his depleted lungs with air. 'I *need*. I need you and this. Tell me you do too.'

His shirt came adrift from the waistband of his jeans as she roughly grabbed two handfuls of the fabric and tugged—hard. 'Of course I do, you idiot!' she hissed as his head came towards her.

'I'm hellish glad you said that,' he breathed as his long, rangy frame came to rest beside her.

The sensuous subtlety with which he unbuttoned her blouse was only heightened by the slight tremor in his long fingers. It made her dizzy looking up at his dark face so Jo closed her eyes. Her breasts strained against the pale pink satin material of her bra, overflowing from the cups. She gave a voluptuous sigh of pleasure as he unclipped the front fastening.

'Will it hurt if I...?'

Jo forced her heavy eyelids open. His expression was as raw as his tone. 'Only in the nicest possible way, Liam.'

He stared in fascination at the way her breasts quivered slightly as a shudder ran quite visibly over her entire body. The pinkness he could recall, quite vividly as it happened, had deepened to a deep coral defining the areola clearly against the creamy pallor of her magnolia skin. The flat of his palms against the outer slopes of her breasts, he pressed gently against her taut, firm skin. With a hoarse cry he suddenly buried his face between the twin mounds and breathed deeply to absorb the sweet feminine scent of her skin.

When he lifted his head her fingers were still pressed against his scalp. 'I could get drunk on the smell of you. I think I *am* drunk on the smell of you,' he reflected thickly. The band of dark colour across the angle of his cheek-bones darkened and beads of perspiration emerged along his upper lip.

Such details were lost on Jo; desire hot and urgent made her incoherent and clumsy. It was as if a great dam had disintegrated at his touch. All the emotions she'd hidden and refused to examine over the past lonely weeks engulfed her.

'Drunk but not incapable, I hope.' Her words sounded more like a plea than a joke. Liam's eyes deepened by several shades when he realised that that was exactly what it was.

'I'll let you be the judge.' Her small hands were cold against his heated skin. Supporting his weight on one hand, he ripped impatiently at the buttons of his shirt and, rolling briefly onto one side, pulled it over his head. 'I can't believe we've wasted so much time.' He was deeply shocked and excited when something as simple as skin-to-skin contact robbed him momentarily of breath.

Jo felt him shudder and she wrapped her arms tightly across his back, enjoying the leashed power in his big body. She didn't know whether his words referred to the recent or more distant past and at that moment it didn't matter. He was here, now, and he was hers!

'I'm afraid I'll…' She heard him mutter against her neck.

'You won't hurt me—us.' She instinctively knew what was holding him back.

He raised his head and Jo couldn't focus—he was too close, his face was a dark blur. She closed her eyes as, weight supported on his elbows, he held her face in his hands. He wasn't holding back when his tongue plunged into her mouth; there was no refined seduction in the gesture, it was raw, unrefined need. A kiss was too tame a term to describe the intimacy of the invasion.

She fought to prolong the intimacy, her body twisting beneath his. Their clothes were shed in a frenzied haste, the process made more difficult by the fact that neither could bear to break the contact that melded their bodies together. The air was filled with soft murmurs of pleasure and hoarse cries of need.

When his fingers slid into the damp, tangled patch between her slim thighs she cried his name in desperation. The piercing need was too great to bear. Liam's voice soothed and coaxed, his touch was delicate and sensuous.

The heel of his hand came to rest on the soft mound at the apex of her legs and his fingers spread out over her lower abdomen. 'It's just incredible,' he breathed. '*You're* incredible.'

It wasn't just his words that cut through the sensual fog that clouded her mind, it was his strange tone. Her eyes, which had been running compulsively over the lean lines of his beautiful body, focused on his face.

Jo saw his eyes were fixed on the gentle slope of her lower belly. They moved upwards to her face. His jaw clenched and a nerve leapt spasmodically in his lean cheek.

'It doesn't get in the way yet.' She lowered her eyes to hide her intense response to his words and carefully placed her fingertips on top of his. Did he notice the slight tremor in her hands?

'There are ways around these things.'

'There are?'

'Trust me.' His mobile mouth lifted at one corner.

'I do.' The reply was swift and instinctive. She couldn't disguise the tell-tale throb in her voice. She didn't know what interpretation Liam placed on it, but the wicked gleam of humour in his eyes faded quite dramatically.

'That's a pretty good place to start,' he said cryptically after a long, thoughtful pause that stretched Jo's nerves to snapping-point.

'Shouldn't you be thinking about finishing?' she remarked boldly. 'I know they say you can't have too much of a good thing, but my sanity is a fragile thing.' Desperation left little room for subtlety and from the way his body stirred and his eyes glittered he enjoyed her candour.

The intimacy of his caresses had brought Jo to the tantalising brink of fulfilment several times already. Her throat was so dry she couldn't swallow, her skin burned and the heavy, hot sensation pooled in her lower body screamed out for release.

'You want this?'

As he slid into her receptive body she let out a low cry. The sense of completion seared her nerve-endings. Her head thrashed from side to side on the pillow. 'Oh, yes, Liam!' she cried brokenly. 'Please!'

'You need me?' he persisted throatily as he pushed deeper inside her, giving her more, but not quite everything. His lips moved against the vulnerable pale column of her neck. 'You want this?' His restraint drove her slightly crazy.

Jo's sweat-dampened palms slid down the curve of his back before coming to rest on the taut curves of his tight buttocks. 'I do…I do… I need you, *always*! I can't bear it without you, Liam!' The words came pouring out; she couldn't seem to stem the wild flow of confessions.

Later, whilst her body was still throbbing with delicious aftershocks of pleasure, she heard his voice close to her ear.

'The vows will come later in front of an audience,' she

heard him say. 'But as far as I'm concerned what we just did was equally binding.'

She rolled over onto her back, her hair spread out around her face like a burning halo. 'What do you mean?'

'I mean, Jo, you're committed to me now.'

'I thought you were serious for a minute.' The carefree laugh was stillborn in her throat as she met his eyes.

'I am serious.'

'I know I said some things, and did some things, but that's just...' Her voice faded away under the harsh displeasure of his expression.

'Did you mean what you said?'

'I can't remember what I said,' she mumbled in horror.

'I can—every syllable. Shall I refresh your memory?'

'You dare!' Realisation swept over her and anger exploded in the confines of her skull. 'You manipulative bastard,' she breathed suddenly. He'd forced her to say all those things deliberately. Held back until she'd bared her soul. She drummed her fists against his shoulders, fighting back the tears of humiliation. How could he be so cold and calculating?

'Could it be you've had total recall?' He caught her fists in his. 'To be on the safe side perhaps I should refresh your memory?' His mouth collided hotly, angrily almost with hers.

What right did he have to be angry? Did he think he could simply kiss her into submission? She tried to ignore the small voice in the back of her skull that told her that was precisely what he could do.

'I don't know what you think this proves. You're a good lover—you're a *great* lover!' she conceded huskily with a sniff.

'We're great together,' he contradicted pointedly.

It seemed that Liam had more on his mind than just

kissing! Jo let out a startled cry as he lifted her bodily astride him.

'You can't!' The fight drained out of her leaving a warm compliance in its place.

'No...?' His hands ran slowly down her flanks, drawing her closer to the evidence that firmly disputed her assertion.

'It's too soon.'

'For you?'

'For you.' He no longer looked exactly angry now, but he did look dangerous.

'Me being a weak, frail male.'

'Past the first flush of youth,' she agreed solemnly.

'Mistake, Jo,' he said, slowly shaking his head from side to side.

'Why...?' she began before he grabbed her by the shoulders and pulled her down on top of him.

'Because I never could resist a challenge.'

Liam proceeded to prove he was up to that particular challenge.

CHAPTER SIX

JO DROVE back into town straight from the final fitting. The local dressmaker had risen magnificently to the challenge of her expanding waistline and the final last-minute adjustments had now been made.

Jo wished she were at the stage when she could have flaunted her 'bump'—she was rather proud of it—but she felt, despite assurances to the contrary, that she looked overweight rather than pregnant. In the cleverly cut gown, people weren't going to assume she was pregnant, but they would nudge one another wondering, Is she? It would give them something to talk about, she thought tolerantly.

The cream silk creation hung in her bedroom waiting for tomorrow morning. Every time Jo thought of the next day she came close to having a panic attack. Though her symptoms were common enough on the eve of a marriage, she was all too aware that the cause of them wasn't!

It was probably a good thing she hadn't had too much leisure to wonder if she was doing the right thing. She'd been drawn into the crazy whirl of preparations in her desire to stop Aunt Maggie over-exerting herself.

She let herself into Liam's flat. They'd decided to spend the last couple of days before the wedding in their respective parents' homes. The Raffertys' place was already heaving at the seams with Raffertys from what seemed like every corner of the globe and her father's cottage wasn't much better. The quiet was welcoming after two days of frenetic activity.

She went straight to the bureau where she'd left her

locket. It had been her mother's and she intended wearing it the next day—*something old* and very precious. She was looking around the room to check she hadn't forgotten anything else when the doorbell rang.

'Hello.' The tall blonde looked surprised to see Jo. It didn't escape Jo's notice that the sharp pale blue eyes didn't appear to miss a detail of her casual appearance. 'Is Liam in? I've been ringing since yesterday. I do believe the bad man has his mobile off.' Her voice had an attractive transatlantic twang and her manner was overpoweringly confident.

It was move aside or be trampled over, so Jo moved aside. 'I'm sorry, he's not here.'

'And you are?' The delicately arched eyebrows rose in the direction of her gleaming hairline.

Jo felt exasperated rather than offended by the older woman's persistence and she couldn't throw off the feeling she'd seen this woman somewhere before. This wasn't likely—Liam's visitor wasn't the sort of person you would forget in a hurry! She was a lady with a lot of presence.

'Jo Smith, I'm—'

'Jo—*you*! Good God, I know who you are, but when Liam spoke about you I assumed you were a guy!' Her startled and not unattractive laughter rang out.

'Easy mistake to make.'

'You must think I'm being very rude.' This realisation didn't stop her examining Jo afresh with overt curiosity.

Jo suspected this woman got away with being a lot ruder than this. She had a way of accompanying her abrasive comments with a disarming smile that probably reduced most men under ninety to compliant jelly. From Jo's perspective a smile didn't compensate for the fact she was being patronised—by an expert, but definitely patronised.

'I thought you were friends.'

'We are friends.'

'Men and women are never *just* friends.'

'No?' Aware that she would be in danger of revealing herself as a hypocrite, Jo kept her mouth firmly shut on the subject. There had been a time when she would have hotly disputed this claim.

The blonde shrugged. 'No offence intended. It's just from the way Liam talked about you I kind of imagined you propping up the bar with him on a Saturday night talking about soccer.'

'I'm more a rugby girl myself, but that's definitely me— one of the boys. I even buy my round.' It wasn't pleasant to be reminded that until recently Liam had treated her so platonically she might as well have been a bloke.

She had had to get pregnant before he'd recognised her femininity. When you thought about it, which she tried not to, it didn't sound a very stable basis for a marriage.

'I need to find him, it's urgent.'

The statement carried the weight of a royal command. This was a lady who was obviously used to seeing people jump through hoops of her own making. Jo didn't feel much like exerting herself. Realising her antagonistic response was possibly visible on her face, she made an effort to smile sympathetically.

'I can give him a message.'

'That's very kind.' The brief smile dismissed Jo's offer. 'But I'd prefer to deal with him directly.'

The implication that she wasn't to be trusted with a simple message tested Jo's forced smile. Perhaps, she pondered, if I'd been wearing one of my smart office suits she wouldn't have dismissed me so readily. The bossy stranger obviously didn't find her denim jacket and baggy sweatshirt confidence inspiring. Perhaps she wanted to pass on more than a message; this probable explanation didn't improve Jo's mood.

'That might be difficult.' Count to ten, don't get bolshy, Jo, she advised herself. It's a bad move to alienate your future husband's friends and colleagues.

She wasn't about to start acting like a paranoid jealous wife just because a good-looking woman was looking for Liam. There were a lot of good-looking women about and statistically it made sense that Liam would know one or two—possibly more.

'Why's that?'

'He's getting married tomorrow.' As one-liners went this was a winner.

The blonde gasped, her heavily mascaraed eyes widening. 'You have to be joking. Please tell me you're not serious.' Under the seamless make-up it was hard to tell but Jo had the impression the older woman had gone pale.

'It's not a joke.' She frowned as a small voice in her head suggested that that was *exactly* what it was—the whole idea of her marrying Liam was a joke in the worst possible taste! 'Liam is getting married.' Liam should be the one saying this, she thought angrily. The woman's reaction had ruled out the possibility they were casual acquaintances. 'I'm sure he will be in touch, Miss…?'

'Suzanna Wilson,' the blonde supplied. 'How could he not mention a word?' She pressed her hand to her mouth as her face tightened. 'When he knows we're near—' She stopped abruptly as a hoarse sound escaped Jo's pale lips. 'Is something wrong?'

Jo shook her head. Not an *old* flame at all. Suzanna. So *this* was the perfect woman Liam had waxed lyrical about in his letters. Strang—she'd had quite a different mental picture.

The name had never been mentioned between them, but

Jo hadn't been able to forget those letters. Suddenly the problem she'd tried to ignore was there in front of her eyes. You could burn letters, as she had, but what did you do when the material proof was in front of your eyes? she wondered despairingly. He'd been seeing her all this time; he must have been. Was that *all* he'd been doing?

She felt suddenly empty inside. What a fool I've been. If I hadn't got pregnant maybe it would have been this woman he'd be marrying. Her fevered imagination was firing on all cylinders as the full horror of the situation made itself felt.

'I said are you all right?'

'Indigestion,' said Jo weakly. 'You were working with Liam in Moscow?' He always did have a thing for older women, she thought bitterly as she stretched her stiff lips into a smile. I suppose she is beautiful, she conceded, if you go for pouting lips, a California tan and long blonde hair. 'I'm sure Liam would have contacted you; his mother's been ill.'

'I wasn't working with him, I followed him,' came back the shocking and unselfconscious reply. 'When I want something I go after it.'

'Obviously.' Did he have this woman's image in his head when he made love to me? When he closed his eyes who was he seeing? Their lovemaking, which had seemed so perfect, suddenly felt contaminated.

'I know his mother's been ill.'

Proof, if she'd needed it, that they'd been in regular contact.

'But that doesn't explain why he's switched his cell phone off. No, Liam just didn't want to tell me he was getting married. He knows—'

'Actually his phone got dropped in a pond.' Jo couldn't

understand what bizarre impulse impelled her to defend him.

'Pardon?' The older woman looked as though it had occurred to her she was speaking with someone who wasn't entirely sane.

'It's a long story. His parents have a lot of children staying.' It suddenly seemed a long time ago that she'd laughed as she'd watched Liam wade into the middle of the duck pond to retrieve his phone; it had only been yesterday.

'Children!' She gave a theatrical little shudder. 'Poor Liam, that must be very boring for him.' She sounded as if she thought he deserved it.

'They're anything but boring. Quite enterprising, actually.'

'But Liam's not really a *children* sort of man, is he?'

'Maybe you're right,' Jo replied heavily. And maybe I don't know him very well at all, she thought despondently. Perhaps she'd been fooling herself into believing he could be content with her and the baby.

'Liam won't be back here tonight, but if I see him…' Even as she spoke she knew she wouldn't be seeing him. This meeting had been fortuitous—it had brought her belatedly back to her senses. Thank God it had happened before she'd done anything irrevocable. 'I'll tell him you're looking for him. It's probably better if I just give you the Raffertys' home number.'

'I didn't know where else to go. Liam will go straight to my flat.' She shuddered as she sipped at the hot drink Justin had pushed into her hands. 'What is this?'

'I put some sugar in…'

'You know I don't take—'

'Hot, sweet tea is the only treatment for shock I know.'

Jo put the cup on the gleaming surface of the walnut bureau. 'I'm not in shock.'

Justin's gaze flickered anxiously to the hot cup, imagining the damage it was doing to the lovingly polished wood. 'I think you are.' He resisted the temptation to move the offending article. 'And I think you're well rid of Rafferty.'

Jo bit her tongue. 'I imagine, given time, he'll think he's well rid of me.' She could understand Justin's antagonism towards Liam; what was less understandable was her own instinctive need to defend him. 'Aunty Maggie sounded so confused on the phone. If anything happens to her he'll never forgive me. *I'll* never forgive me.' Her fingers tugged fretfully with the hem of her baggy top and her eyes were dark with misery. 'I just can't go through with it,' she whispered huskily.

Justin patted her awkwardly on the back. 'The man has coerced you shamelessly into a marriage repugnant to you. If anyone should be ashamed it's him! It was moral blackmail.'

Jo was already regretting giving Justin even a strictly expurgated version of events. 'Coercion is a strong word, and I'm not actually married.'

'Thank God for that!' Justin glanced down at the Rolex on his wrist. 'I really hate to leave you like this, but my flight's booked for ten.' He looked torn.

'Don't be silly, I'm fine. I just need somewhere to hole up until the heat dies down. I would have gone to a hotel, but I didn't have my wallet with me and I couldn't risk going back home for it.' If she'd seen firsthand the results of her last-minute change of heart she might not have had the strength to go through with it. 'I'm such a coward.'

'I'm glad you came to me. Don't worry,' he added drily, seeing her uneasy expression. 'I know it was desperation that brought you to my door, not a change of heart. I've accepted you don't feel *that* way about me.'

'I'm sorry, Justin. I wish…' Her voice trailed away. I seem to be an expert at hurting people these days, she reflected gloomily. Guilt ate away at her as her face creased with concern. 'I shouldn't have come here; it was selfish.'

'Nonsense, I'm glad you came.' He slid the hot teacup onto a coaster and was relieved to see no damage on the antique wood. 'I just wish I could have seen Rafferty's face when you told him. Did you phone him or…?'

An unusually spiteful expression flickered over Justin's handsome features and Jo realised that Justin's warm hospitality was inspired as much by dislike of Liam as love of her. The realisation eased her remorse.

'Not phone, exactly.'

Justin picked up his bag and looked towards her questioningly.

'I faxed him.'

Justin turned away to hide the grin of uncharitable delight that spread over his face. 'Faxed. How…enterprising. I'll have to go now, Jo. Stay as long as you need. I'm back on Monday.'

Alone once more, Jo couldn't concentrate. She flicked blindly through the TV channels. With the soothing voice-over of a wildlife documentary playing in the background, she began to pace the room. Jilting someone was a terrible thing to do and the closeness she felt to the Raffertys made matters even worse.

They'll probably hate me, she concluded morosely. Her elbow caught one of Justin's prized antique figurines and with a gasp of dismay she straightened it. Justin's flat was dauntingly neat—even his glossy magazines were stacked with military precision. She found herself automatically comparing it to the simplicity of Liam's decor. For a brief, wildly blissful moment it had been her decor, her home. She'd started thinking in terms of *us*, not him and me. They'd discussed the house they would buy together.

'Stop it!' she reprimanded sharply. Seeing Suzanna had put paid to that fantasy. She wanted to spend her life with Liam, she wanted it so much that she'd managed to turn a deaf ear to the unpalatable fact she had virtually trapped him into marriage.

For his own reasons he was a willing victim, but that didn't make him any less the victim. Maybe the awful Suzanna wasn't his soul mate—*she hoped not*—but one day there would be one and Jo knew that she couldn't bear to witness the inevitable disintegration of their makeshift relationship.

Better by far to accept now that Liam was no longer part of her life. How hard could that be?

When she first heard the key in the lock Jo assumed Justin had forgotten something, which was not like Justin at all. The poor thing would have missed his flight. She was about to call out when she heard a voice most unlike Justin's. It was much deeper and had an intriguing gravelly twang.

'Thanks a lot. I didn't want to wake her.'

Jo's feet seemed frozen to the spot. Her hands went to her mouth as she stared at the open doorway.

'You!' she gasped as the tall figure materialised on cue. 'How…?'

Liam didn't speak immediately. He took his time looking around the room, allowing Jo ample time to appreciate the full awfulness of the situation. 'Very tasteful,' he said nastily.

'Go away! Be careful with that!' she yelped as he picked up a small bronze and turned it over.

'A good fake.'

'So now you're an expert on antiques too. How did you know I was here?'

'I didn't. I knew you didn't have a penny to your name. That limited the possibilities.' He threw her wallet containing her credit cards on the sofa. It fell open and her spare change scattered messily. 'Hotels were obviously out. I rang every number in your address book and no joy.' He was breathing deeply as he raised his eyes directly to her face for the first time.

'How dare you go through my personal belongings?'

'I dare because you walked out on me without a word of explanation on the eve of our wedding.'

Liam was mad, my God he was *really* mad. The air in the room was dense with the sort of static that a thunder storm carried in its wake. He was carrying his own personal storm around with him. Jo had a fanciful image of him opening his clenched fist to reveal the flicker of blue lightning. He was nursing a deadly sort of anger. It made his voice low and calm and all his actions slow and deliberate as though he had to force himself to concentrate hard on the little things.

'Guess who popped up in your little black book? By some twist of fate your trusty old flame, Justin. What's wrong—is his telephone number as forgettable as the rest of him?' His nostrils flared as he smiled nastily. 'When I saw him driving away my first thought was, No, she's not here. What unimaginative idiot would leave the woman he loves in an emotionally vulnerable state? What sort of man would walk away from a situation fraught with possibilities?'

'Not all men take advantage of vulnerabilities.' Jo knew the insinuation wasn't entirely fair, but she experienced a perverse pleasure when the lines of tension radiating from his mouth tightened.

Liam's white, even teeth came audibly together in a white, cruel smile as he replied. 'More fool them.'

'How did you get in?'

'Easily, once I explained to the doorman that my wife and I—he might have seen her earlier: short redhead, pregnant—were staying at Justin's. You shouldn't think too badly of him.'

'I don't. I know what a good liar you are.' Could he see she was shaking? She locked her fingers together and pressed them against her midriff to hide the fine tremors.

'You're too kind.' The fake smile faded away. 'I think we've about exhausted the story of how I got here. What shall we talk about now?' He frowned exaggeratedly as if seeking inspiration.

'I don't want to talk to you at all, Liam. Go away.' Jo wasn't entirely surprised when he didn't. She didn't dare speculate where this encounter was leading. Damage limitation was the best outcome she could hope for.

'We could always discuss this.' He produced a piece of paper which he flung in her general direction. 'Nothing quite beats the personal touch. I suppose I should be grateful you didn't just leave me standing at the altar.'

'I wouldn't do that!' she gasped. She bit her lip with anguish as he poured scorn on her assertion with a quirk of one eloquent eyebrow. 'I understand you're feeling a bit upset but—'

'*Upset!*' A dark rush of colour seeped slowly under his tan as he gazed at her with icy contempt. 'That's very understanding of you, Jo.' He bit the words out from between clenched teeth.

'I know a fax is a bit impersonal,' she conceded shakily.

'But I knew that you'd talk me out of it,' she admitted, cornered—the truth was the only way out.

'You being such a pliant, impressionable soul,' Liam sneered, unimpressed by her honesty.

Ironically he had no idea just how impressionable she was as far as he was concerned. 'You being a totally unscrupulous bully,' she retorted, forgetting in the frustration and heat of the moment that she was going to be sensitive and reasonable. 'Besides, I *want* to marry you—that is,' she pushed on hastily, 'it would be much *easier* to marry you. Easy but not *right*.' It sounded a bit priggish and limp even to her ears.

'Last night it was right. This morning when I spoke to you on the phone it was right. What's changed?'

'I wasn't thinking straight.' For some reason Jo couldn't tear her eyes from the throbbing pulse in his temple.

'Why change the habit of a lifetime?'

'It couldn't last, Liam.'

The desolation in her tone seemed to penetrate his fury. Stern blue eyes searched her face and his anger didn't dissipate, but it was now leavened with a seething frustration. He covered the intervening space between them and took her by the shoulders. She had the impression he wanted to shake her, but he didn't.

'There are never any guarantees, you know that, Jo.' He wasn't handing out concessions; the planes of his angular face held no softness, just fierce determination.

'I don't want guarantees,' she retorted, 'just a fighting chance.'

He flinched as if her words had caught him on the raw. The truth always did hurt, she reflected woefully.

'And you don't think we have that?'

She shook her head from side to side and then as a great wave of desolation swept over her leant her forehead on his arm. She felt his fingers tighten on her shoulders. He shifted his shoulder and his arm came around her bowed head, drawing her face against his chest.

'You've never even considered marriage—at least not to me.' Her voice was muffled against his jacket. He smelt so good—if only she could stay like this for ever, she thought wistfully. It felt so *right*.

'Not to anyone.'

'Not even Suzanna?'

'Who?'

Jo lifted her head, her eyes alight with indignation, and Liam's arm fell away. 'The Suzanna you wrote pages about in your letters.' At least before Liam had always been straight with her.

'Oh, that Suzanna,' he said a shade defensively.

'*That* Suzanna.' Well might he look shifty. 'I met her today.'

'What? That's not poss…'

'She came to the flat this morning looking for you.'

'Typical,' Liam mused, and Jo was disgusted to see a faint ironic smile curve his firm lips. Was breaking women's hearts all in a day's work for him?

'I'm afraid I told her you were getting married,' she choked. 'She wasn't very happy.'

'I can imagine, but she'll survive.'

'Liam!' she gasped, shocked at this heartless response. She looked at him searchingly. Was he trying to mask deeper feelings behind this callous exterior?

'What's wrong?'

'You can't just discard people,' she told him severely. 'It's…it's ruthless.'

'Are you in any position to comment? Some people might categorise your actions as ruthless. Ruthless, uncompromising, selfish...' he added, just in case she'd missed his point.

The irony was something she couldn't, under the circumstances, share with him. Giving Liam his freedom was probably one of the most selfless acts she'd ever be called upon to perform; she certainly hoped so! An undisciplined part of her wanted to fling accusations at him... It's me you're supposed to love!

'Are you in love with Suzanna?' She wouldn't allow him to deflect her from the subject. Perversely she sought out confirmation that would hurt.

'No.'

This categorical denial didn't make her feel much better. 'You used to be honest with me,' she muttered, raising reproachful eyes to his face.

Liam sucked in his breath sharply. 'I don't know why you bothered asking me if you've already made up your mind.'

'In your letters you—'

'Those letters were...' Jaw set, he turned his head away from her for a moment and muttered something inaudible under his breath. Jo caught the tail-end of 'too clever for my bloody good.'

'Were what?' she prompted. 'Other than gushingly sentimental, that is.'

'I am never...' His eyes suddenly narrowed and a slow, disturbing smile tugged at the corners of his mouth. 'My God! Is that what all this is about? You're jealous.'

Jo stiffened. 'In your dreams, Rafferty,' she croaked. 'I just don't like being treated as your social secretary by your latest girlfriend.'

'You hated the idea of me with Suzanna so much you did a runner.'

She longed to slap that satisfied smirk off his face. How

dared he find her pain and humiliation amusing? 'Under normal circumstances, Liam, I have nothing more than an academic interest in what female is deluded enough to share your bed. However, as I was wearing this damned thing...' she glared at the big emerald and tugged at it without any real belief her efforts would achieve anything; it seemed nothing short of surgery would dislodge the thing '...it occurred to me that it might be uncomfortable to be married to someone who comes home at night smelling of someone else's perfume.

'In the past I've always been tolerant of your sexual exploits. However, in the past I wasn't expected to share your bed. Possibly you get some sort of kick out of discussing your sordid affairs—I believe some people do. However, I'm not prepared...' It was a mistake to look directly into his eyes; she saw sizzling anger there and completely lost the thread. 'No...no, I'm not,' she faltered before losing steam completely.

There was a moment's shocked silence, though the echo of her shrill accusation still seemed very loud in the quiet room. 'Just what sort of arrangement do you think I had in mind when I proposed to you, Jo?' He didn't give her space to reply but went on in a soft, deadly voice that throbbed with anger, an anger that was reflected in his harsh, taut expression. 'We both lead our own lives? You thought you could go running back to your old lover when it suits you and I would turn a convenient blind eye...?'

'It wasn't like that!' she gasped. He couldn't think she and Justin were taking up where they left off!

'Like hell it wasn't,' he said with a tight-lipped smile. 'I can see the tender scene now.' It didn't look as if he was enjoying what he saw. 'And I'd like to make it quite clear right now that I take great exception to the idea.'

He took...! At what point had the tables been turned?

she wondered numbly. She almost expected to hear herself humbly apologising—*never*! The nerve of the man! What right did he have to come over all morally superior? She quivered with moral indignation.

'The thought of incurring your disapproval has me trembling,' she assured him with heartfelt insincerity.

'I'd noticed.'

She glared up at him. Damn him, did he miss nothing? 'That's anger,' she hissed.

'If you say so.'

'Don't you *dare* humour me, Liam Rafferty!'

'Considering the picture you've just so eloquently painted of an inadequate who fancies himself as a sexual athlete, I think you owe me some leeway, Jo. If we're to trade insults on a one-for-one basis, that is.'

Jo could feel the hot colour wash over her skin. 'I didn't say that exactly.' Hearing it put like that made it hard to maintain her belligerent pose. 'Besides, don't all men do that with their mates in the pub—talk about their sexual conquests? It must have really cramped your style when you had me in tow.' The idea of Liam thinking of her as one of the lads made her want to stamp her feet. It was very frustrating being too mature to indulge in this childish outlet.

'Cramp my style? What the hell are you talking about, Jo?' Liam asked, running his fingers through his thick mop of hair and watching her with an expression of exasperation.

'*She* thought I was a man.'

Liam's mystified frown gave way to a grin which he swiftly stifled. 'Suzanna?' he enquired gravely as he pushed back a hank of dark hair that had flopped in his eyes.

'Who else?' She hadn't missed, or forgiven him for, the grin.

'I suppose I might have mentioned you a few times, and when she asked I think I probably said you were my best friend.' Liam looked up as she sniffed rather loudly. He silently handed her a handkerchief from his pocket. 'She must have assumed…'

'People don't marry their best friends,' Jo said heavily. 'They're normally the wrong sex.'

'This isn't about gender.' He could be flippant while her heart was breaking—there was just no justice in the world! 'This is about love and sexual chemistry. It isn't fair to ask either of us to sacrifice our—'

'You expect to find love and sexual chemistry *here*?' Liam interrupted scornfully.

'I'm not about to marry Justin.'

'Too right you're not.' His eyes narrowed to slits and he thrust his hands deep in the pockets of the khaki chinos he wore. The action drew her reluctant attention to the narrowness of his lean hips and the length of his thighs.

This had to be some sort of punishment for all the times she'd always thrown scorn on women who were turned to marshmallow by a brooding look, she decided, desperately trying to quell the strong urge to throw herself into his arms and babble brainlessly about his beautiful blue eyes.

'Because *I* don't want to.' Her chin took on an aggressive angle as she gave him back stare for stare even though she was handicapped by knees that had turned to jelly.

'You said you wanted to marry me.'

God, the man had the recall of a computer! 'I said—' she tried hard to sound calm and reasonable, but she felt neither,'—that it would be *easier* to marry you.'

'I wouldn't have thought it would be easy being married

to a man who intends to sleep his way through the female population of the Western hemisphere.'

'Why stop there?' she snapped, sensing he was backing her steadily into a corner. She knew him too well to underestimate his tenacity.

'I'm immensely flattered at your opinion of my sexual prowess, but I think perhaps you're not quite as objective about the subject as you might be.'

'And what,' she enquired icily, 'is that supposed to mean?' Please don't let him know, she prayed. Let me retain a little dignity. The fear of discovery was a bitter taste on her tongue.

'I mean that, despite our lack of sexual chemistry,' he drawled slowly, 'the past couple of weeks we spent together were pretty hot.'

'Hot,' she echoed stupidly. She felt weak with relief; for once Liam hadn't recognised the obvious. 'There's no need to be crude.'

Liam laughed. 'If you think *hot* is crude, sweetness...'

'I am not your sweetness.'

'Granted, but I've always preferred something with a bit more bite.'

'I don't enjoy trading sexual innuendoes with you.'

'Does this blanket disapproval cover sharing sex with me too? Are you going to tell me you didn't enjoy the time we spent together?'

'When you say the time we spent together I think you're actually talking about the time we spent together in bed.' She tried to inject scorn into her voice.

'I've certainly enjoyed that part.'

The husky sound of his voice aroused her body with shocking ease. She folded her arms protectively across her aching breasts.

'In these enlightened times people don't get married to

have sex, no matter how—' She broke off as she realised what she'd been about to say. From the expression on Liam's face he realised it too.

'You were saying?' he taunted heartlessly.

'I was saying that sex is no basis for marriage.'

'Are you trying to say you want to carry on sleeping with me, but you don't want to marry me?'

'No!' she cried in a shocked voice.

'It sounded suspiciously like it to me.' She watched with misgiving as his lazy mocking expression was replaced by something much more steely. 'We're good in bed—scrub that, we're *great* in bed. My relationship with Suzanna Wilson is nothing that need concern you. I've no intention of sleeping with her or anyone else once we're married— my God, if the time we spent together is anything to go by I'd have no energy,' he added half to himself.

'Well, you didn't seem to mind at the time!'

'I didn't mind at all.'

This devastatingly simple reply made her whimper. Biting her own tongue was a crude method of breaking the spell of his eyes, but desperate circumstances didn't allow time for finesse.

'I obviously didn't make myself clear earlier—I don't want a cosmetic marriage,' he told her huskily.

She could taste the salty tang of her own blood on her tongue. 'No?' It was hard to maintain her scepticism in the face of such solid conviction.

'Most definitely not.'

'And does it matter what I want?'

'We've already established that you would find it easy to marry me.' He moved swiftly on as she opened her mouth to challenge this assertion. 'The same goes for our sexual compatibility, or,' he enquired with a quirk of one darkly defined eyebrow, 'were you faking it?'

'As I said, that's hardly a basis—' she began, this blush sort of merged with the earlier ones which hadn't faded yet.

'You're carrying my child,' he interrupted smoothly, 'and that child needs both parents.'

'Piling it on thick, aren't you, Liam?' she choked resentfully. 'Aren't you going to lay your mother's failing health at my door too?' Everything he was saying made perfect sense. Was she just greedy for wanting more than he was offering?

'Mum's strong enough, that needn't come into the equation. I shouldn't need moral blackmail to make you see we should get married. On your better days you're a reasonably rational soul.'

She gave a disparaging grunt. 'You've changed your tune!'

'However, you do realise that once your dad gets wind of this he'll probably come after me with his shotgun.'

'Don't joke,' she advised darkly. 'You're still only fractionally above Attila the Hun on his list of people he'd like to break bread with.'

'Who's joking? And I can understand how he feels—he thought you were safe with me.'

She could see that the distaste in his eyes was aimed at himself and it hurt. 'Aunt Maggie will probably already have told him.' One of these days she'd actually think of the consequences before she acted impulsively. Liam had got it in one: she'd run away because she was eaten up with jealousy. The sort of knife-twisting, stomach-churning jealousy she hadn't even dreamt existed.

'No, I convinced Mum it was just a case of last-minute nerves. Apparently you were pretty unintelligible on the phone.'

'I was...' She looked away avoiding his eyes.

'Blubbing,' he finished knowledgeably. 'Mum mentioned that. I know it bothers you that we're not madly, passionately in love.' Jo hardly noticed that it was his turn to look uncomfortable and avoid her eyes.

'I...never imagined it this way,' she admitted huskily. 'Marriage, I mean.'

'I intend to take my vows seriously, Jo. You'll never have to worry about other women. I respect you too much.'

'Respect.' She clamped her lips together; suddenly she was spitting angry. 'I don't want respect, I want...' Hands clenched into fists, she pressed them to her mouth and closed her eyes.

'What?' His fingers touched the side of her cheek. 'What do you want, Jo?' There was a greedy urgency in his soft voice as he bent over her.

I want you to love me. For one heart-stopping second as their eyes met she thought she'd actually said it. Frightened by the suicidal desire she had to tell him the truth, she scrabbled to her feet.

'Ouch, sorry,' she gasped in dismay as he backed away, his hand clamped to the lower part of his face. When he moved his hand she saw the blood on his lip. 'I didn't mean to... Are you all right?'

'Bruised, but not beaten. *Am I?*'

Her throat was too engorged with emotion to permit speech. When had Liam ever admitted defeat? she thought wearily. She couldn't run away from him any more than she could run away from her own feelings. She knew at that moment that she would marry him the next day. She couldn't consider the subject objectively—she was just responding to a deep gut instinct that told her it was something she *needed* to do.

'If it's Suzanna that's bothering you I can explain—'

'Don't!' She lowered her voice. 'Please, I don't want to

know.' Ignorance wasn't bliss, but it was more bearable than the unvarnished truth.

He shrugged. 'As you like,' he said, his expression unusually guarded. 'We *can* make it work.'

Jo believed he would never betray her, not in the physical sense. She respected that, but fidelity of the heart wasn't something a person had control over, as she knew all too well. It was unbearable to think of him wanting someone else and being tied to her. She couldn't lose his heart because it had never been hers.

'I don't like pretending.'

'Then don't.'

If only. A weak wave of longing swamped her; she was getting good at disguising such things. 'It feels…awkward when you act as though we're a couple in public.'

'We *are* a couple.'

She shot him an exasperated look. 'You know what I mean, the…touching and so forth.' She fumbled awkwardly for words. 'It's really not necessary, when people are bound to realise we're only getting married because of the baby.'

'A lot of people get married because of a baby, but it's not usual for them to act as if they're strangers,' he said, effortlessly tearing her tenuous logic to shreds. 'When I touch you privately or publicly it isn't to fulfil a role. I do it spontaneously because I want to…'

'Oh!' she gasped, meeting his direct angry blue stare with wide-eyed confusion. Don't read anything deep and meaningful into it, she told herself. Liam always had been a very tactile person. He'd always touched her—that hadn't changed, it was her reaction to that touch which had undergone a transformation.

'And because I thought you liked it,' he continued softly. 'Are you trying to tell me you don't?'

The question made her start guiltily. 'I...I just didn't want you to feel obliged,' she floundered. 'To act a role.'

His eyes narrowed thoughtfully. '*I'm* not having any trouble acting normally. You're the one who can't relax. Nobody expects you to drool over me and hang onto my every word as if—'

'I expect that's what you're used to, but I've no desire to ooze or drool,' she grated from between clenched teeth.

'Then what's the problem? You're just not the type. When you and Justin were pretty full on you never went in for extravagant displays of—'

'I save my displays for behind closed doors.'

Liam couldn't stop his mind placing Jo and Justin behind a closed door. His jaw set hard. 'What I'm saying is even if you were...'

'In love with you,' she finished crisply. It was easier to throw scorn on the notion herself than hear him do it. 'What insight, I'm impressed. And you're the expert on the soft, drooly type of female, I assume. Speaking as the hard-boiled, unemotional variety myself I'd be really interested to hear more. For your information I was devastated when Justin left me.'

'I recall,' he said in an oddly expressionless voice. When her eyes collided with his he looked inexplicably angry. 'I'm not saying you're hard-boiled,' he continued, 'just...emotionally objective.'

'If I hit you over the head with a blunt object it will comfort you no end to know I considered the alternatives objectively.'

'This is much better,' he approved.

'What?' she yelped, bosom heaving.

'Be yourself,' he advised her calmly. 'I'm much more comfortable with you throwing insults, or even assorted missiles at me than being all jittery and polite.'

She mentally reviewed her behaviour and a frown developed over the bridge of her nose. 'I haven't been that bad. Have I?' It was true—she did feel as though all her actions were under a microscope. Deceit always had made her uncomfortable and what had started off as a small lie had grown out of control. Not only did she have to act like a loving fiancée for the benefit of others, she had to disguise the true state of her feelings from Liam. A complicated double bluff like that was enough to make anyone jittery!

'Worse,' he confirmed. 'Nobody expects you to undergo a personality transplant before marriage. Forget about the impression you're giving. We're comfortable with one another, Jo, that's what people have often mistaken for intimacy. And now we are intimate... Wouldn't you have missed that if I'd let you run away?'

His long eyelashes left a dark, delicate tracery across the slant of his cheek-bones as his eyes dropped low to run slowly over her body. The husky sound of his voice had a debilitating effect on her nervous system, and he knew it, damn him!

'Don't push it, Liam, you've sold it. I'll be at the church tomorrow.'

Liam was gracious in victory, he didn't crow at all. He pushed her belongings back into her shoulder bag and handed it to her. 'Let's go, I can't stand this place.' For some reason he glared murderously at the closed door behind her.

'I should leave a note for Justin, he'll—'

'We'll send him a fax; you know how to do that.'

CHAPTER SEVEN

'WHAT was that, Niamh?'

The older woman smiled knowingly at the vacant, dreamy expression on the bride's face. 'I was asking if you're still being sick?'

Jo gathered her drifting thoughts and smiled at Liam's sister. Her pregnancy, never a secret, now seemed to be the property of the world and his sister. She'd heard enough scare stories from mothers today to make her wonder why most of them had gone through this ordeal more than once in most cases.

I'm married, I'm *really* married. It didn't seem real somehow. She couldn't dispel the impression that the entire day had actually been some elaborate surreal dream; any minute now she'd wake up.

'It was terrible with Liam—it went on until I was seven months,' the brunette confided ghoulishly. 'Though it was better with Brendan.'

'I've been fine the past few weeks, thank goodness. I'm a bit tired, though. Actually I thought I might just slip away and change. Do you think anyone will notice?'

'I shouldn't think this lot would notice an earthquake,' Niamh observed, looking around the crowded marquee with an indulgent smile. She held up her wine glass. 'And no wonder—every time I empty this some nice young man fills it up.' She grinned with approval. 'I think Liam's already made a break for it. Are you two going away somewhere nice?'

'Actually Liam's got work commitments. This is all a

bit of a rush job.' Jo wished she could stop sounding so defensive every time someone asked her about their non-existent honeymoon.

'Rush!' Niamh's uninhibited laughter rang out; the Raffertys were an uninhibited sort of family. 'Most people think you and Liam have been pretty slow getting to the point. Still it's a shame about the honeymoon,' she commiserated. 'What is it, sweetheart?' she asked as a tow-headed four-year-old clambered onto her knee.

With a smile Jo made her escape as Niamh's attention switched to her young son. The hem of her long gown gathered in one hand, she reached the covered walkway that had been constructed between the marquee and the house having only been stopped by well-wishers five times. She welcomed the coolness as the canopy above her head billowed and flapped in the breeze as she hurried along.

She hadn't expected to enjoy the day but surprisingly she had. From the moment her father had woken her with a cup of tea she'd felt as if she were on the outside watching, and this sense of detachment still hadn't diminished. It was some stranger who had calmly recited her vows and posed for the interminable photographs.

The jury was still out on whether she'd lost a friend to gain a lover, but one fact was unalterable: she'd definitely gained a husband. That realisation ought to have been enough to give substance to the day's events, but it wasn't.

The study door wasn't closed as she passed, and hearing the sound of voices she automatically slowed down. Despite the fact a medium had once authoritatively told her all the females in her family were blessed, or cursed, with strong psychic ability, Jo didn't feel even a prickle of precognition as she paused long enough to hear the sound of Pat Rafferty's deep voice.

'I'm not sure I expected it to go this far, son. I mean, I wasn't thinking too straight when your mother was ill.'

'There's no need for you to feel guilty, Dad.'

At the sound of Liam's voice Jo began to unashamedly eavesdrop. She let go of the banister and took a step backwards, straining to catch the rest of the conversation.

'I connived with you to blackmail that girl into marrying you. I'd say that's something to feel guilty about! Pass me one of those cigars and don't tell your mother I've had one. She thinks I've quit.'

'I doubt, Dad, that Mum thinks anything of the sort.' Jo heard the clink of glasses. 'Shouldn't we call it a day, Dad? Too much of this stuff has a tendency to make you maudlin.'

'True enough, your mother's got eyes in the back of her head, but it's a little game we play. She pretends she doesn't know about my crafty drags and I pretend I don't know she knows.' Pat's soft brogue thickened as his voice broke emotionally. 'You traded on that girl's love of this family, boy.'

'Jo walked up the aisle today of her own free will.' Liam's deep, steady tone was confidently strong. 'I'm not saying the fake engagement didn't give her an opportunity to get used to the idea.'

'I care about Jo, Liam. I agree it's a bad thing when the law gives an unmarried father so little say in how his child is brought up. I understand your anger and concern.'

'The scales are certainly weighted in favour of the mother,' she heard Liam agree. 'But, Dad, that's—'

'Of course I wanted you to marry Jo. Secretly I think your mother's always hoped it would happen...'

'Possibly that's why it never did. Mum's not that subtle.'

'That's as maybe, but marriage is a pretty drastic step

to take just to ensure you have a legal say in your child's future.'

'Hold it there, Dad...'

Her hands were clamped over her ears as she pressed her back to the wall for support. She couldn't move until the waves of nausea and shock passed.

Part of Jo's brain was furiously denying what she was hearing even as another part was meticulously weighing all the damning evidence that said it was the truth. All along Liam had made no secret of his repugnance at the idea of the man of her choice bringing up his child. If she thought about it logically, what other reason could explain his complete about-face on the subject of marriage? One minute he came out in a rash at the very suggestion and the next he'd embarked on a relentless campaign to get her up the aisle.

She knew he wasn't in love with her, she'd told herself she could cope with that—but this? Was all this to gain legal, unarguable rights over this unborn child? All that talk of security and a stable environment had been a smokescreen for his real grand plan. She placed a protective hand over her belly. He'd been preparing the way for when they weren't together.

There was something so cold and calculating about the way he'd set about achieving his goal, and *deceitful*! If nothing else, she had always implicitly believed in Liam's honesty. The knowledge her trust had been terribly misplaced cut deeply. She felt betrayed and humiliated.

She'd thought they had a common aim—to make this marriage work. When in reality it was just a means to an end as far as he was concerned! Her dreams had been recklessly creative and until this moment she hadn't known how strongly she'd come to believe that something stronger would grow from their warm friendship. Like an

idiot she'd staked everything on this foolish, irrational belief.

She wasn't aware of the despairing cry that emerged
from her throat as she picked up her skirts in both hands
and ran up the stairs.

'Jo!'

She ignored the sound of Liam's voice and just concentrated on reaching the bedroom door. The thundering
sound of her own blood pounded in her ears. She could
hear the sound of his footsteps behind her getting closer
and closer.

'Stop it! What are you doing?' Liam pushed his foot in
the doorway as, panting, she tried to close the door in his
face. He set his shoulder to the door and she felt herself
being pushed steadily backwards. To resist him physically
was pointless, she knew this, but obstinately she gritted
her teeth and refused to give up. For some reason even her
token resistance was important.

The door was wide open and Liam was in the room
before she gave up. 'Go away!'

'Are you trying to kill yourself?'

'Your concern is touching,' she spat sarcastically.

She looked at him directly for the first time and Liam
visibly recoiled from the animosity in her luminous eyes.
'I don't know what you heard…' he began cautiously.

'How inconvenient.'

'This is…I thought you'd realised.' His fingers closed
over a hank of his freshly trimmed hair and left it standing
up spikily above his brow before he began to rub his chin
against the palm of his hand. 'I wanted to tell you, but I
wasn't sure how you'd react.'

'Well, now you know.' Hands on her hips, she faced
him, her bosom straining at the ivory lace.

'It was a shock?' A grey tinge had spread over his

healthily tanned skin which pulled taut over his strong bones, making it look as though he'd suffered a shock himself.

'Silly me, hey! For some strange reason I thought I meant more to you than a...a...walking incubator!'

His big body froze and his dark brows drew together abruptly in a straight line. *'What?'*

'I told you I never intended denying you a full part in bringing up the baby. As far as I was concerned it was always going to be a fifty-fifty split—in those days I thought you were the sort of man who any child would benefit from having as a father.' She gave a scornful laugh and swallowed a sob of self-pity that welled in her throat. 'But my word was obviously not good enough for you. You wanted it all legal and binding and you didn't care how you did it. Well, I swallowed it hook line and sinker... I actually thought you genuinely believed we could make a go of it.'

'My God, *that's* what you heard.' Bizarrely he laughed. 'You mean there was worse?'

'I suspect that depends on your viewpoint,' he said, his lips twisting into a thin smile full of self-mockery.

Jo didn't understand his peculiar expression; she just knew she was hurting. If he looked a bit as if he'd been run over by a runaway truck, it was just because her discovery of his true motivation was an inconvenience—he'd already got what he wanted, she told herself bitterly!

'It's not what you think, Jo.'

'Now why,' she sneered sarcastically, 'aren't I surprised to hear you say that?'

A flicker of anger passed over his face. 'How long do you intend indulging in this orgy of self-pity?'

Jo let out a startled squeak of outrage. 'Don't try and turn this around, Liam Rafferty. I'm not the one who—'

'I am not trying to turn anything around,' he interrupted in a harsh, impatient tone. 'I'm just trying to get you to shut up and listen to me for one minute.'

'Oh, you'd like that, wouldn't you?' She'd done enough listening to Liam to last her several lifetimes. 'Save your breath, Liam, nothing you can say can alter what you've done.'

'What exactly have I done?' There was deliberate provocation in his tight-lipped smile. The spark of anger in his eyes was beginning to show signs of smouldering.

'You can ask that?' she choked in disgust.

'Quite the drama queen, aren't we?' His expression hardened. 'I'm not about to act the guilty party for your benefit, Jo.'

'I know what I heard,' she said stubbornly.

'*Part* of a conversation...'

'Which only got worse, by your own admission.'

'If you'd take that sneer off your face and let me get a word in you could be the judge of that.'

She shook her head dismissively. 'I suppose you think a court would give you custody. How long did you give this marriage: three years? One? You're so big on forward planning you've probably got the legal team picked out for the custody battle.' And he'd have a battle! How naive she'd been to think Liam's vows had been a long-term commitment.

'Good God, woman, the child isn't even born yet! But,' he continued in a goaded voice, 'if they could see the unbalanced way you're acting now...'

'How dare you imply I'm an unfit mother?'

'Motherhood has nothing to do with it, you've always been the most pigheaded female I've ever met. Totally incapable of seeing more than one side of any argument.'

'This isn't a debate.'

'No, just a witch-hunt.'

'Are you going to deny you couldn't bear the idea of Justin bringing up your child?'

'I'm not going to deny it—why should I? No man in his right mind would want that dummy as a role model for his offspring. But the personality, or lack of it, of your ex-lovers has nothing to do with this.'

'No, it's my future lovers you were worried about.'

'There aren't going to be any future lovers—you married me, remember.'

'Well that,' she snapped tugging the gold band from her finger, 'can soon be remedied.'

He instinctively ducked and the ring flew over his head. 'What are you suggesting? Divorce?' he suggested sarcastically.

Standing there in his black jacket and pinstriped trousers with his tie pulled loose at the throat, his hair standing on end and a dark shadow already developing over his jawline, he looked just about the sexiest, most gorgeous male to ever draw breath. I even find his scorn seductive! Acknowledging this disastrous circumstance made her aggressively furious, and just a little desperate.

'Fine!'

'What did you say?' he said in a quiet voice that she'd never heard before. Jo had thought she was familiar with every intonation in his repertoire.

'I'm saying…' What the hell am I saying? she wondered. He wasn't alone in being shocked by the words that had defensively emerged from her lips. Her chin went up defiantly as, pushed to the brink, she couldn't bring herself to back down even though a small voice in her head warned her she was making a big mistake. 'I'm saying I don't want to be your wife.'

'Be careful, Jo.'

'The time to be careful was yesterday. Now I've just got to retrieve what I can from a situation which has frankly become distasteful.'

Liam's head reared as her words struck home and the sound of him sharply inhaling was audible. 'Distasteful...' he mused slowly. There was a white line etched around the sensual outline of his lips. 'An interesting and evocative choice of adjective.'

'I never wanted to be your wife.' Part of her wanted to stop but the impulsive words continued to spill from her lips. 'I was bullied and cajoled into thinking it was the best way.' Liam had hurt her deeply and her instinct was to hit back and come out of this situation with a modicum of her pride intact.

His expression froze and a frostily blank expression slid into his normally expressive eyes. 'Then there's nothing else to be said.'

That was it? She couldn't believe her ears. His reply made her feel as though a dark hole had opened up at her feet. She knew her response was perverse—she hadn't fallen into an unseen obstacle, she'd dug the hole and jumped in! She was getting what she wanted, wasn't she?

Liam *always* argued, his tenacity was legendary! She certainly hadn't been nursing a deep-seated fantasy that called for him to produce some flawlessly logical explanation that would soothe her fears. Her stomach lurched sickeningly as the implications of his capitulation sunk in. Obviously he didn't think it was worth fighting over. He was probably *relieved*.

'I think it will be easier for everybody concerned if we leave—together, without mentioning your decision.'

'What...?' she said blankly. He sounded so objective and in control. How *dare* he cope so well when her world was collapsing around her ears?

'It would be kinder to break this to our families on a more private occasion. Do you think you can manage that?'

'They'll be confused...' She bit her trembling lip and tried not to think about the emotional fallout she'd have to endure. She walked over to the window to hide the tears that suddenly welled in her eyes.

'*They'll* be confused?'

Devastated was probably closer to the truth, she thought bleakly. Married and separated all on the same day; could this be some sort of miserable record? Jo pulled off her veil and let it fall to the floor. Liam's irony was wasted on her; she was still feeling disorientated and dazed by the speed with which things were happening.

'And whose fault is that? You let me think we both wanted the same thing from this marriage.' She had no intention of shouldering full responsibility for this situation.

'I *hoped* we would eventually both want the same thing from this marriage, but you've made it perfectly clear that I was a fool to imagine—'

'I don't know what you're talking about,' she interrupted angrily.

'I'm well aware of that.'

She was getting heartily sick of his cryptic little digs. 'There doesn't seem much point in having a conversation if you insist on talking *at* me, not to me.'

'I didn't think I had to talk at all. You seem able to tell me what I'm thinking without me even opening my mouth.'

'You opened your mouth all right, you just didn't know I was listening.'

'Eavesdropping.'

'So sue me,' she snapped, yawning elaborately.

'So sorry if I'm boring you.'

'We do seem to be covering the same ground repeatedly.'

'I don't know why I ever thought this would work.' Liam regarded her with intense dislike.

I don't care if he doesn't like me, I'm *glad*, she told herself belligerently. She couldn't let herself pause long enough to think about how much she *did* care; it would be too painful. Right now, whilst her emotions were hot and unpredictable, she could blot it out, but later it would be different.

'The problem was it didn't matter that much to you either way.'

'Do you think you can resist calling me a callous, manipulative bastard until we get clear of this fiasco?'

'Duplicity doesn't come as easily to me as it does to you, but I'll try,' she promised with a glare that carried almost as much animosity as his.

'I leave you alone and look what happens.' Claudia leaned back in her seat and caught the waiter's eye. 'Another one of these,' she said, indicating her empty glass, 'and a double orange juice for my friend. What's happening over there, Paolo?' She indicated an area of the restaurant to their right where there seemed to be a lot of activity.

'They've been interviewing some hotshot writer,' he said, adopting a confidential manner, 'and they're taking some photos now. I can move you to another table if you prefer, Miss Raphael.'

'And rob us of a glimpse of someone famous? No chance.' Claudia laughed. 'Don't you just love nepotism?' she observed happily. 'If Uncle Guido didn't own this place we'd never have got a table. I just love celebrity spotting.'

'The food's not bad either,' Jo responded, smiling at her friend's enthusiasm.

'I'll pass on your compliments to the chef. From the way you're picking at that zabaglione I'd assumed it wasn't up to standard.'

'I'm not very hungry.'

'Then hand it over. It would be a pity to waste it.' Claudia had a very relaxed attitude towards calories and no hang ups at all about her generous curves.

'How is Justin?' Jo asked. Claudia and Justin worked in the same chambers and it was through him they'd first met. The two women had hit it off straight away.

'He worries about you.'

'Don't!' Jo pleaded. 'I feel guilty enough as it is. He was too nice for me.'

'Yes,' Claudia agreed thoughtfully.

'Pardon?' Jo shot her a startled look.

'I didn't mean that quite the way it sounded. I just never actually thought you and Justin were particularly well suited.'

'You never said.' Jo felt a little put out by this revelation.

'You never asked.' She pushed aside her empty dessert plate and placed her chin on her steepled fingers. 'Pregnant, married and working on the divorce—I still can't believe it.'

'When you say it like that it does sound...'

'Hasty?' Claudia suggested.

'Not you too. I've had it up to here—' Jo banged her forehead with her fist '—with people telling me I'm behaving irrationally.'

'Calm down, Jo, I'm not about to lecture you. In fact what I actually want are some of the gruesome details. Why else would I bring you to a very exclusive restaurant?

I want the warm Mediterranean ambience to chip away at all those Anglo-Saxon restraints—let it all hang out. You'll feel much better and I'm much cheaper than a therapist; neither do I have the meter running.'

'How can I resist an offer like that? And here I was thinking you only brought me here because your uncle owns it and he doesn't charge you.'

'Don't be picky, spill the dirt. Did you really never, *ever* sleep with the delectable Liam until the night Justin dumped you?' she asked incredulously. She smiled and shrugged as Jo's eyes opened wide in indignation. 'No need to look so scandalised. I always assumed that... I mean, it's pretty unusual... The only men I'm *that* friendly with are my ex-lovers—at least, some of them.'

'That accounts for your legions of *friends*.'

Claudia smiled complacently, quite unruffled by this insult. 'You should meet my mother, you'd get on. She wants me to stop behaving badly, get married and produce babies. Now, about Liam...'

Jo gave a sigh of exasperation. The dogged characteristics that made Claudia such a good lawyer made her an exasperating friend sometimes. 'You and Justin are friendly but you were never...' Jo blinked '...*were you*?'

'No, of course not.' Jo had never seen her friend blush before. A sudden suspicion entered her head.

'Well, are you going to tell me?'

The sharp question distracted Jo from the revolutionary idea that had occurred to her. 'Tell you what?'

'Tell me what the delicious Liam—'

'I do wish you'd stop saying things like that,' Jo interrupted crossly.

'Things like what?'

'Delicious and delectable...'

'Fine, what did your unattractive and nondescript husband do to make you do a runner on your wedding night? I should tell you opinion differs on this one, but I lean towards the unnatural sexual practices theory. Justin thinks it was another woman—or, rather, women.'

'I'm glad my private life provides the legal profession with a little light relief.'

'Come on, Jo, don't get all bitter and twisted—you know we care about you. You must admit, it does give rise to speculation when a girl jilts the groom after the ceremony.'

Foolishly the genuine warmth and affection in Claudia's brown eyes made her own grow misty. 'I knew he was only marrying me because of the baby, but I thought he believed our marriage could work.' Disastrously her voice began to quaver.

'And he didn't believe that?'

Jo blew her nose defiantly. 'No, he just wanted to make sure he had rights—legally—over how the baby is brought up. It was a cold, calculating plan.'

'Says who?' said Claudia sceptically.

'Says him... I mean he said so, I didn't invent it, I heard him! He doesn't give a damn about me.'

'I've always had the impression Liam gives several damns about you. In fact I have this theory...'

'This is the part where I'm supposed to say, What theory?' Jo was a little piqued that Claudia hadn't recoiled in shock when she'd revealed the awful truth; lacking that, sympathy would have been nice. She had obviously failed to see the enormity of Liam's crime and she didn't seem to appreciate that it would be impossible to trust him ever again.

'Liam's always shared everything with you, but his body—right? All his deep inner feelings and equally profound emotions? At the same time he has been a very popular boy with the ladies, but not exactly renown for his staying power. You see, he didn't *need* anything deep and meaningful from them because he already had that with you. Are you following me so far? Don't worry if you're not, I'll be quite happy to answer questions at the end.

'The thing is, once the sex thing reared its ugly head and you two swung from the chandeliers—I take it we are talking torrid with a capital T here?'

Jo shifted uncomfortably and hoped the subdued lighting was disguising her high colour. Claudia was suddenly very handy with the questions, she thought resentfully, but she wasn't hanging around waiting for answers, which on reflection might, under the circumstances, be a blessing! Her photographic recall of every occasion upon which they'd made love was proving quite a handicap. The last thing she needed was Claudia's help to resurrect the memories which were never far from her thoughts.

Claudia rubbed her hands, warming to her theme. 'Whammo, he has the intellectual, friendship bit and the lust all wrapped up in one convenient parcel. He doesn't need other women; he has you.' She placed her elbows on the table and looked smug. 'What do you think?'

'I think if you look to your right you'll see a slight flaw in your theory.' Her own voice sounded as though it were coming from a long way off as it competed with the thunderous sound of the blood pounding in her ears.

'What...?' Claudia twisted around in her seat.

'A five-foot ten flaw, with flowing blonde hair and a cleavage that defies all laws of gravity,' Jo elaborated in a composed tone that didn't even hint at the knife that was twisting away at her vital areas. 'She's just walked in the door—with Liam.'

'That's Suzanna Wilson!' Claudia gasped. 'And it's a push-up bra not gravity you're seeing there—I'm wearing one myself,' she confided, twitching her silk shirt and giving anyone interested a view of her lacy undergarments.

'I know that's Suzanna Wilson—how do you?' Pregnancy obviously caused softening of the brain—for a minute there she'd actually thought Claudia's theory ranked along with that of relativity. I'm not just pathetic, I'm *stupid*!

'Are you kidding?'

'You mean she's famous?' That figured; it certainly explained the air of consequence.

'Famous! Where have you been living, Jo? She's the most bankable female director in Hollywood, which means in the world. You must remember when she was slated by the feminist press for her last film—they called it exploitative and degrading. It was also wildly profitable so I don't think Suzanna is losing too much sleep. Is it all coming back to you?' She looked rather anxiously at her friend who didn't seem able to tear her anguished gaze from the tableau. 'How do you know her, Jo?'

'I know her as the woman who came looking for Liam...the woman who followed him to Moscow. The same woman Liam described in some letters as a cross between Joan of Arc and Marilyn Monroe.' Abject misery was being kept at bay by a full-blooded fury. He hadn't wasted much time.

'Didn't both those ladies share a certain vulnerability?' Claudia shook her head slowly. 'I'd say our Suzanna is armour-plated, but men do tend to see these things differently—especially when they're not thinking with their brains, if you know what I mean!'

Jo knew *exactly* what she meant. The idea of Liam doing any of the things, the glorious, blissful things, he'd done to her to that...that...! She couldn't be sick, not here! She laughed and Claudia looked at her anxiously.

'What's wrong?'

'I actually felt guilty the last few times I refused to take his calls,' she recalled bitterly. 'Jessie painted a picture of a broken man who might do something desperate. Even allowing for Jessie's sense of the dramatic I thought he might be feeling unhappy.' Unhappy was the least he could do under the circumstances. 'Well, whatever remedy Suzanna carries in her handbag it seems to have done the trick.'

'Hell! Now I know why I went into criminal law, not family,' Claudia observed miserably. 'Crime is relatively straightforward. Just as well you don't take any notice of my theories.'

'Isn't it?' Jo wasn't about to admit that she had been quite entranced by the picture Claudia had painted. Entranced to the point where she'd been ready to bare her soul and her true feeling to Liam.

'She puts something quite literal into the term "in your face". Don't you think?' Claudia observed, grimacing as the blonde slid her arms around the man she stood behind and leant forward to smile seductively up into his face.

'Liam doesn't seem to mind.' It was almost as if he heard his name.

'He's seen you!' Claudia hissed. 'Follow me, I'll take you out through the kitchens.'

The sympathetic looks and angry sympathy that accompanied her through the noisy kitchen made Jo quite glad she hadn't understood the content of Claudia's rapid explanation in Italian.

Emerging at the back entrance of the restaurant, she was breathless. She placed her hands on her head in an attempt to tame the fiery nimbus of curls which had gone a little wild in the steamy atmosphere.

'Let me get my breath,' she panted, leaning forward and bracing her hands against her thighs.

'If Liam tries to go through there he'll get a very unfriendly reception.' Claudia laughed, rubbing Jo's shoulder. 'Are you all right?'

'Fine.' She shrugged away the concern impatiently. 'What did you say to them...? They won't hurt him, will they?' A vision of Liam's beaten and bruised body floated horrifyingly before her eyes.

'It's nice to know you care.'

'Delegation is all well and good but sometimes nothing beats the personal touch.' Chin up, she managed to act as if the sight of him leaning nonchalantly against the metal barrier that shielded the small alcove at the rear of the restaurant from the car park hadn't sent her nervous system into a frantic state of total chaos. 'I don't want to talk to you, Liam.'

'I'd never have guessed.'

'Won't your friend be missing you?'

'I expect she'll find something to amuse herself with. Suzanna's very resourceful.'

'I'm so pleased the reports of your mental collapse were wildly overstated,' she said, sounding anything but pleased. 'It's good to see you haven't been bored. No, don't go!' She grabbed Claudia's arm.

'I'm not going far, I'll hear you if you yell.' She shot Liam an unfriendly look. 'I don't think I should be hearing this.'

'My thought exactly.' Liam's nostrils flared as he recognised the panic in Jo's green eyes.

'Your thoughts are of no interest to me,' she snapped, glaring at him.

'Why does Claudia think you'll need to yell? What exactly have you been telling her about me?' His languid pose, which hadn't been very convincing to begin with, faded completely.

'The truth would do, don't you think?'

'Your version of it, I assume.'

'Don't come over all innocent and misunderstood with me, Liam Rafferty—not after that little display in there.'

'I'm promoting my book.'

'Nice work if you can get it,' she hissed nastily.

'I'm working on the screenplay. Suzanna's production company are making the film. She's directing.'

'It looked to me like she was participating. Incidentally, I don't think that shade of lipstick is really you.'

Liam pulled his fist across his lips. 'I'm learning from an expert...' his eyes narrowed in anger before his eyelids drooped suggestively over the twin lights of cynical blue '...at self-promotion.' His smile held the cruelty their friendship had once protected her from.

'I didn't think you wrote fiction, I thought you just spouted it.'

'I'm not really interested in discussing my career. Talk to me, Jo,' he grated urgently.

'Why? Nothing's changed, except you're being less discreet about your outside interests—don't worry, I'm not complaining. As far as I'm concerned you can sleep with anyone you like, you're a free agent.'

He looked anything but pleased by this magnanimity. 'I'm married.'

'You should be grateful you don't have to go on pretending.'

'I never pretended with you, Jo.' He moved closer and she automatically inclined her head to maintain eye contact. 'I didn't have to.' He placed a finger to the vulnerable line of her soft lips. 'Why won't you believe me?'

'I should have known it would turn out like this after I

slept with you.' Even knowing this, she felt every fibre of her being crave his touch. Forcing herself to acknowledge this fatal flaw in her make-up was very hard. 'I've seen the way you operate with women, Liam.' She would find ecstasy and misery in Liam's arms; she had to be strong and deny herself one in order to protect herself from the other.

'Meaning…?' Underneath the dangerous calm Jo sensed the submerged, explosive anger.

'You've never made a concession in your life towards the women you've dated. It was always on *your* terms; they had to do all the running. *They* had to compromise, and when they did you promptly got bored.'

'I wasn't married to any of them.'

'You forget I know why you married me.'

'As a matter of fact you have no bloody idea! And the only running you've been doing is in the opposite direction. Didn't the vows you made mean *anything* to you, Jo?'

'How dare you ask me that?' Her voice quivered with outrage. 'That ceremony was just a means to an end as far as you were concerned. It must have been a drag having to tear yourself away from Miss Wonderbra ninety-eight!' She was too distraught to conceal the jealousy that was eating her up.

'This has nothing to do with Suzanna, or the baby.' His eyes flickered almost greedily over her body, noting the changes. 'It's all about the fact you don't trust me.'

Green eyes glittering coldly, they swept dismissively over him as her lips curled into a scornful smile. 'And I never will, Liam.'

Her words were like walking into one brick wall too many. Nothing he could say or do seemed capable of breaking past this barrier she'd built to keep him out.

Something inside him snapped. He moved forward and, one hand behind her head, the other around her waist, he hauled her bodily off her feet and covered her mouth with his.

Her startled cry was swiftly cut off by his ravaging mouth; her arms hung limply at her sides as he devoured her soft, unresisting lips. The cry had been enough to bring Claudia running.

'Don't worry, Claudia.' Liam was panting as though he'd been running and his colour was heightened as he turned stiffly to face her. He couldn't look at Jo; the sound of her lost cry was going to haunt him for a long time. All he'd done was live up to her expectations of him. 'You won't need to scream for reinforcements. I'm going.'

The kiss had been an outlet for his anger and frustration—the shame twisted like a knife in his guts. No wonder she looked devastated. A quick glance had taken in her desperate pallor and wide, shocked eyes. His own lack of discipline revolted and sickened him.

'Perhaps it's actually your feelings you don't trust, Jo, not me!' God, I haven't even got the guts to admit I'm in the wrong, he thought in disgust as he turned away.

The words had been a pure defence mechanism. If he'd looked back he'd have been amazed to see the effect they'd had on his wife.

'I'm sorry, Jo. No wonder you didn't want to be left alone.' Claudia placed a comforting arm around her friend's shoulders and glared with distaste at the tall retreating figure. 'Liam always comes across as so civilised and...' She shook her head. 'It just goes to show you never really know.'

'You don't understand, do you, Claudia?' Jo said in a flat, expressionless voice. 'I didn't want him to stop.'

CHAPTER EIGHT

'I FEEL terrible letting you down like this.'

'You're not letting me down,' Jo said firmly. Claudia did indeed look the picture of guilt. 'I'm quite capable of coping with a parent-craft class on my own.' Since she'd moved back into her old flat—luckily she'd not given up the lease—she'd coped with most things on her own.

On this occasion, despite her self-sufficiency, Jo's heart secretly plummeted at the idea of mingling with all the couples in the class. Her solitary state made her feel conspicuous at the best of times, but at least with the support of Claudia she had someone to laugh with. Nobody else seemed to see the funny side of several heavily pregnant women and their partners puffing obediently away whilst they visualised a summer sky.

She sometimes thought that she ought to have chosen a class with a slightly less whimsical approach to childbirth. Still, the classes were informative, even if she did feel a little out of her depth when people started talking knowledgeably about birthing pools, home births and acupuncture, and on the whole she enjoyed the evenings.

Nobody, it seemed, had looked at her quite the same way since she'd mentioned the possibility of pain relief. It wasn't as if she had anything against natural childbirth, she just wanted to leave her options open. If she'd announced her baby's father was a Martian nobody could have looked more shocked than they had when she'd said her birth plan was *flexible* and she hadn't actually got around to writing it yet!

'You'll have nobody to rub your back.'

'I expect Cynthia will oblige.'

Claudia bit back a grin. 'You must hate me,' she said with dancing eyes.

Cynthia was their *very* serious tutor. She was stuffed full of New Age philosophy, had a sweet personality and very high expectations of her pupils. Jo was gloomily certain that she was going to prove herself a disappointment.

'I just wish she wouldn't call me "chick".' Jo wrinkled her nose. It makes me feel like I'm back in kindergarten.'

'Tut-tut...' Claudia shook her head. 'You're meant to feel an empowered woman with control of your own body.'

'It's all right for you to joke.' Jo placed a hand over her swollen belly. 'I don't feel in control of anything, even my bladder. Have you any idea how often I had to get up last night and go to the loo?'

'Come off it, you're thriving on it!' An untypically coy expression flickered over Claudia's face. 'Are you trying to put me off the joys of motherhood?'

'Don't tell me *you're* contemplating...' Jo couldn't disguise her amazement; Claudia was the epitome of the self-sufficient thirty-something career woman. She carried a laptop not a baby—but then some people had probably said the same of me a few months ago, she reflected philosophically.

'Not immediately...but who knows...?' she mused with a mysterious smile guaranteed to fuel Jo's curiosity.

'You didn't breathe a word. Who's the lucky man?'

'Did I say I've lined up a stand-in for me tonight?' Claudia said casually.

'No, you didn't, but don't change the subject.'

'Actually I'm not, it's Justin, and he's agreed to come and breathe heavily with you tonight.'

'You and Justin!'

'You mind! I hoped you wouldn't.' Claudia looked crestfallen.

'No, of course I don't mind,' Jo responded swiftly as she recovered from the shock. If I hadn't been so self-absorbed I'd have put two and two together already. 'I just didn't know you two were…you know…an item.'

'An item might be too formal yet.' Claudia looked relieved at the unaffected sincerity of Jo's response.

'How long have you…? I mean, did you like him when I was…?'

'Actually, yes, but he didn't spare me a second glance back then.'

'Oh, Claudia, I'm so sorry.'

'Don't worry, I'm going to get him on the rebound. I think he likes me a little bit.'

'If you got him to agree to go with me to an antenatal class he must be besotted with you! You did warn him what it's like?' Her eyes widened at Claudia's self-conscious grin. 'Claudia, that's very bad of you. Poor Justin.'

'I'm hoping it'll turn him all broody.'

'You are the optimist, it's more likely to turn him cat-atonic!'

That was how she ended up, against her better judgement, squatting on a rush mat with Justin supporting her as she panted obediently alongside ten other large ladies. Actually Justin had surprised her—apart from blushing when he'd been referred to as 'Dad' by the redoubtable, sandalled Cynthia, he'd coped remarkably well.

A saint couldn't have coped with what happened next so she forgave Justin for letting her slip in an untidy heap on the mat. The door abruptly opened; the noise as it banged against the wall broke everyone's concentration.

'I think, young man, you've got the wrong room.'

'No, I haven't.'

'Liam, what do you think you're doing?' Jo was suddenly conscious that she was now sharing the attention which until that moment had been reserved solely for the tall, dark, dangerous-looking stranger. Indignation was warring with a lot of less manageable emotions in her chest.

'I need to talk to you.'

'This isn't the time or place.'

'Where is? You won't take my calls. You rip up my letters unopened...'

'How...?'

'I still have some allies in the Smith household.'

Jessie—she'd kill her! That must be how he knew she'd be here tonight, the little traitor, had she never heard of sisterly solidarity?

'As you can see, I'm busy. I'm sure this can wait.' Her tone of lofty dismissal was wasted on Liam.

'I can see how that might suit you,' he sneered.

'And what is that supposed to mean?'

Liam looked beyond her. 'Take your hands off her, Wood, *now*.' He sounded casual, but the expression in his eyes had their leader reaching for her mobile phone; up to this point she'd been just as engrossed as the rest of the class by the heated discussion.

'If you don't leave this instant, young man, I shall be forced to contact the police.' She tried belatedly to compensate for her passive state.

'I've every intention of leaving...'

'Then we'll say nothing more of this interruption.'

'With my wife.' Liam looked directly at Jo.

The dramatic pause was timed to perfection; all around her Jo could hear the mumbled exclamations and shocked whispers. She could of course call his bluff and refuse to budge, in which case Justin might feel obliged to make a gesture he'd definitely live to regret. Or she could go with Liam and use the opportunity to tell him exactly what she thought of this sort of stunt.

She got to her feet with as much dignity as her bulk would permit. 'No, don't get up, Justin. Claudia's due to pick us up straight after class,' she whispered. 'You might as well wait for her—I'm sure you'll learn a lot.'

'Will you…?'

'I can cope with Liam.' She wished she felt as confident as she sounded. She patted his shoulder. Justin wasn't comfortable with the situation but, as she wasn't exactly being dragged kicking and screaming from the building, there wasn't a lot he could do. 'Sorry for the disruption, Cynthia.'

'No harm done, my dear. Mr Smith…' She raised her voice and her eyes to Liam.

Liam tore his stunned eyes from Jo. Standing up, the ripe fullness of her new shape was very apparent. Jo was rather proud of her shape even though the restrictions it placed upon her were irksome sometimes. Her chin went up; if he didn't like it—tough!

'Rafferty,' Liam corrected shortly. The knowledge she was going by her maiden name brought a fresh disapproving twist to his lips.

'Mr Rafferty, we encourage fathers to attend our classes.' Justin went bright red as her eyes travelled from Liam to him and back again. Liam's expression was carved in stone.

'Yes, I am.'

Cynthia dissolved into embarrassed confusion. 'Really I wasn't…I never pry…'

With a sardonic smile Liam closed the door.

'I hope you're satisfied!' Jo exploded. 'I'll never be able to go back there again. I can only assume that your intention was to humiliate and embarrass me.' She turned her back and stalked off down the corridor.

It took Liam about two strides to catch up with her. 'Like I said, I want to talk to you. The humiliation was by way of being icing on the cake, *Mrs Smith*.'

'Ms. It was Jessie, wasn't it, who told you I'd be here?'

'I never reveal my sources. Now I can see why you didn't want to talk to me—you were too busy patching things up with that feeble excuse for a man.'

Let him think what he liked, especially if it was something he *didn't* like, she thought spitefully. 'Justin is a caring, sensitive—'

'Like I said, feeble. He let me take you—'

'You didn't take me anywhere, I came. You might have dramatic inclinations but I don't! How corny can you get, charging in there like some wronged husband?' she scoffed.

'At least you remember I am your husband.'

'I'm working on that.' She threw a smile over her shoulder just to show how well she was coping with seeing him again for the first time in…the fact she could recall to the hour how long it had been was a depressing give-away.

'Watch the steps,' he cautioned, catching hold of her arm.

Jo shrugged off his restraining hand. 'I'm pregnant—not ill,' she said pointedly.

'Jessie told me you had gone to antenatal class with a friend. She didn't say it was *him*. How long has this been going on? I have a right to know!'

'If you carry on grinding your teeth like that your dentist is going to make a fortune out of you.'

'We're not discussing my dental work!' he bellowed, abandoning his tight-lipped control with a vengeance.

'I know, I was just offering a bit of friendly advice.' She smiled with sweet insincerity. 'We were discussing your rights—you don't have any. End of discussion. If only everything in life were so straightforward.' She sighed.

'That's enough, Jo.'

Jo looked very pointedly at the hand he had placed on her shoulder. Her lips pursed when he met her withering glare and didn't remove it.

'Last time we met I shouldn't have...' To her amazement he looked embarrassed. 'I won't kiss you,' he said abruptly.

She wasn't particularly surprised he felt confident enough to make that particular promise—she was hardly likely to inspire lustful thoughts in her present state! 'With this...' she looked downwards '...you couldn't get close enough.' In her dreams, the ones she'd woken up from, her body soaked in sweat, he'd been able to kiss her. In those dreams he hadn't stopped kissing her before she'd been able to respond.

'You can't avoid the issue by being belligerent.'

'After you've just humiliated me in front of the entire class and insulted my friend I think I'm entitled to be belligerent.'

'You've only yourself to blame that I had to resort to extreme measures. You've cut yourself off from everyone; your father's worried sick.'

'The last I knew he wasn't talking to you.' When the crunch came men always closed ranks, she decided resentfully.

'Which shows you how long it is since you spent any time at home.'

'I've been busy.'

'Doing what?'

'I need to expand my client list. That doesn't happen magically, it requires a lot of hard graft.'

'I'm not questioning your intentions, just your timing. Do you really think that it's appropriate to be traipsing all over the country when you're eight months pregnant?'

'That's something I discuss with my obstetrician, not nosy, interfering strang—'

'If you call me a stranger, Jo, so help me I'll…' She watched his big hands clench and unclench at his sides as he stared down at her with an expression of overwhelming frustration.

She could see how he might want to throttle her. So what if she was being deliberately provoking? She had cause—the instant she'd laid eyes on him her hard-fought-for tranquillity had crumbled like a house of cards faced with an intrusive draft of cold air. He could have no idea—she clung to that small, inadequate crumb of comfort. No idea that the longing was a live thing, clawing and pulling at her insides. Cutting him out of her life totally hadn't been a petty act of vengeance, it had been about survival! Anger was the only thing that kept the debilitating weakness under control.

'Did you have to come barging in?' she asked huskily.

'I had intended waiting outside until—'

'You saw Justin go in with me! Typical!' She sniffed.

Liam didn't deny her version of events. 'Is he proposing to hold your hand during the birth?' he enquired stiffly. A dull red colour ran up under his olive skin.

'Heavens, no!' she responded without thinking.

'That's something, I suppose.' She sensed the explosion of revulsion that had seemed imminent was delayed rather than cancelled by the horror in her voice. 'You can't carry

on shutting me out of this,' he continued in a driven voice.
'When I saw you looking like that it brought home just
how much I've missed.' His eyes strayed to her swollen
body. Revulsion would have been easier to deal with than
the fascination and flicker of awe she saw there.

Empathy was wildly misplaced in this situation and she
frowned with irritation at her own instinctive response to
his gruff protest. 'And whose fault is that?' she asked bitterly. '*You* complicated things. If you'd left well alone and
trusted me we wouldn't be in the middle of a divorce.
We'd still be friends!'

'I hate to shock you but marriage and friendship are not
mutually exclusive.'

'They are when you find out your partner is a callous
bastard who couldn't be straight if his life depended on it.
I'm not getting in there,' she added as they reached his
parked car. 'You can't make me,' she told him as he
opened the door of the dark Mercedes.

'You're not *that* big,' he murmured comfortingly. 'And
it's a very spacious car.'

'I'm glad you find something amusing in this situation.
Pardon me if I don't fall down laughing.'

'If you think I find it amusing that I've missed out on
half my wife's pregnancy…'

The expression she glimpsed in his eyes as she automatically glanced at him made her feel an inexplicable
surge of guilt. There had been such *loss* there… 'Your
mother knows what's been happening with the…'
Awkwardly feeling strangely self-conscious, she placed
her hands over her belly. 'I thought she'd…'

'She did,' he said shortly. He reached inside the breast
pocket of his jacket. 'She gave me this.' He took out a
well-thumbed grainy black and white print which Jo immediately recognised.

'The scan,' she whispered.

'I should have been there, Jo.' His voice was flat and his eyes bleak.

Jo bit her lip. She'd known he'd mind but—*that much*? The doubts that usually afflicted her in the middle of the night suddenly came flooding in. She didn't have to justify her decision, she told herself. It was *his* fault.

'You can keep it, I don't mind,' she said huskily.

'Going soft on me, Jo?'

'Any more smart remarks and I won't take a lift home.' She slid into the plushly upholstered pale leather interior, busily rationalising her decision. After all, she had to get home somehow, didn't she? And, being very ultra-sensitive to smells at the moment, she avoided public transport whenever she could.

'Are you all right?' As he belted himself in Liam noticed her wince.

'Fine, I've just had this niggling backache all day. It's nothing. Did you know that trains smell of burning rubber? That a lot of cabbies wear the most terrible aftershave and stale tobacco smoke lingers for ever?'

'No.'

'If you'd ever been pregnant you would.'

'Are you trying to tell me I smell?'

He did—absolutely marvellous. Naturally she didn't share this information. 'I was just making conversation.'

'Anything to avoid the issue.'

'I thought it might do you good to realise pregnancy isn't all soft-focus pretty stuff. Lots of husbands have a pretty hellish time.'

'What am I supposed to say? Thank you for sparing me? Do you really think I'm the sort of immature clot that only wants to be around for the nice bits? Just when I think I

know how low your opinion of me is you go and say
something illuminating.'

'I'm just saying…' The depth of his anger was pretty
shocking.

'I know what you're saying. Did it ever occur to you
that I've been worried about you? I can see it didn't,' he
added with a grim smile as his eyes flickered from the
windscreen. 'I don't suppose it occurred to you either that
I might like to be around to help you through the less
picturesque patches of pregnancy. Damn it to hell, that's
all we need!'

Having just pulled onto the motorway, they had to come
to a dead stop behind a queue of traffic. Liam's fingers
drummed impatiently on the steering wheel and on cue the
rain began to fall, just to add the finishing touch to the
situation.

'It could be worse.'

'Tell me how!' Liam drawled sarcastically.

'This backache might not be a backache.'

Liam's mouth was open to form the cutting riposte that
was on the tip of his tongue when the implication of her
hoarse comment sunk in. Jaw slack, he swivelled around
in his seat. 'Tell me that's a joke in very bad taste—
please.'

'I'm not laughing,' she pointed out shakily.

'You can't, it's too early.' He'd gone almost as pale as
her.

'Tell him that, not me,' she suggested, nodding towards
her belly.

'Don't panic,' Liam said, running a slightly unsteady
hand through his hair.

'I'm not,' she squeaked, grabbing hold of the dashboard
as the wave of pain low in her abdomen gripped her once

more. 'It was worse this time,' she gasped as she sank back in her seat.

'It'll be fine.' The strained expression in his eyes didn't quite mirror the calm certainty in his voice. 'You are *sure* you're in labour?'

'Sure! How can I be sure? I've never done this before! Maybe it's a false alarm, but if you don't mind I'd prefer to err on the side of caution!'

'Calm down, breathe.' He had the definite impression breathing and childbirth were inextricably linked. Breathing and hot water—he couldn't supply the hot water.

'I am breathing,' she told him, not displaying much gratitude for this guidance. 'Get me to the hospital, Liam.' She closed her eyes, feeling somehow confident that Liam would get her out of this situation. She wouldn't have her baby in the middle of a motorway traffic jam—she couldn't! She opened her eyes as the car suddenly began moving.

'Are we supposed to drive on the hard shoulder?' she asked as a cacophony of car horns followed their progress.

'Do you want me to stop?' Liam asked as, grim-faced, he sped along.

'I think that might be a good idea.' Liam didn't respond; he too had seen the flashing lights of the police car in his rearview mirror.

CHAPTER NINE

LIAM rolled down the window with an expression of impatience rather than dismay.

'Would you like to get out of the vehicle, sir?' With an expression of world-weary cynicism that said he'd heard all the excuses, the uniformed officer pulled on his cap.

This was just one straw too many. He couldn't have Liam—not now, *she* needed him.

'No!' Jo pleaded, her voice shrilly penetrating with panic. 'Don't leave me, Liam!' She clutched his thigh in a vice-like grip as another wave of pain hit her. She didn't hear what Liam said to the policeman, but a few moments later the passenger door was opened. Jo gave the officer a look of wild-eyed panic as her composure cracked completely.

'Don't you worry, we'll get you to the hospital. We're only fifteen minutes from the City, Miss…Mrs…?'

'Rafferty,' Liam supplied, pulling Jo's head onto his shoulder and running a comforting hand down her neck.

'I can't be having the baby, it's too soon.' Lifting her head, she felt frustration as the two men exchanged glances. 'I haven't packed my bag,' she added as though this not insignificant fact clinched the argument. 'Or written a birth plan.' Her teeth wouldn't stop chattering. 'I'm booked into St Catherine's for the birth not the City.'

'Under the circumstances I don't think they'll turn you away,' Liam assured her drily.

The policeman straightened up, his radio in his hand. He spoke briefly before his head reappeared. 'I'll follow

162

you, sir. A motorcycle will lead the way. Don't you worry, my dear, this happens every day.'

'Not to me!'

Their escort didn't desert them when they left the motorway but continued on through the urban sprawl to the hospital. Later Jo would only recall the hazy impression of flashing lights reflected against the wet windscreen and the moan of sirens—her senses were concentrated on what was happening inside her.

Liam kept up a casual flow of soothing comments as he drove along, but his knuckles stood out white against the steering wheel. His career had taken him into some hazardous situations and dangerous places, it had even got him thrown in jail once in an unfriendly country. Give me war zones and inhospitable natives any day, he decided as the feeble attempt he made to make her smile fell flat—and no wonder, I sound like an imbecilic game show host!

'Sorry.' He'd never felt so helpless in his life.

'No, don't stop, it helps.'

'It *does*?'

'I'm scared, Liam. What if...?' The fears she didn't want to acknowledge darkened her eyes; she couldn't push them back any longer. One part of her saw the hospital lights with relief, another part was terrified by the inevitability of it all. Nine months—or in her case almost eight months—should be long enough to prepare herself, only it wasn't.

'It'll be fine, Jo, and tomorrow all this part will be a bad memory.'

The confidence in his deep voice helped her regain control. 'I guess it's too late to change my mind now.' Her pale lips formed a feeble smile.

The room which had been full of people for the last half-hour had suddenly emptied and she was left, clad in a white hospital gown with only the steady drip of the intravenous infusion to keep her company. The door was open and she could hear what the doctor was saying to Liam as they paused outside.

It occurred to her as she listened to Liam ask another question that he knew an awful lot about the nitty-gritty of childbirth. She hadn't thought to ask half so many questions. Part of her had just been relieved to hand the responsibility over to someone else. Even when they had explained something she'd found it hard to concentrate on what they'd been telling her.

'So labour has stopped?'

'Temporarily.'

'How temporarily?'

'We can't leave it too long. There's a danger of infection once the membranes are broken...'

'Danger...Jo's in danger?'

'Mr Rafferty, your wife is fine, and the likelihood is she'll go into labour spontaneously very soon. A few hours can make a big difference to a neonate's lung maturity. Six weeks premature is not unusual and although the baby is quite small for dates...' The doctor's voice faded as they moved away.

A few minutes later Liam reappeared at her bedside. 'Did you hear all that?'

'Most.' She flushed, oversensitive to what she suspected was a reference to her recent habit of listening at doors. A few times over the past weeks she'd wished she'd never heard those fatal words—words that had changed everything. She despised herself for craving ignorance in her weaker moments.

'You should sleep. Do you mind if I stay?'

He *wanted* to stay; for the moment she didn't want to delve any deeper into this satisfying discovery. Knowing he wanted to was enough to light a warm glow inside. His body was tensed against rejection—she knew him well enough to see how much her reply meant to him. She didn't have to weigh the pros and cons of her response, it was instinctual.

'If you try to get out of that door I'm likely to throw an earth-shattering tantrum,' she told him gravely, doubting if he would realise this claim wasn't much of an exaggeration. 'I need someone in my corner,' she admitted distractedly, not noticing the flare of emotion in his blue eyes. 'Every time someone in a white coat talks to me I find myself nodding my head like an idiot. At the moment I could well agree to a brain transplant. Don't say it...' she warned huskily.

The tension drained out of him almost visibly. 'I won't say anything if you don't want me to.' He took a seat without taking his eyes off her pale, drawn features.

'I didn't plan it this way, Liam.' The memory of how things had been meant to happen were fast fading. She could live without a tape of her favourite classical music and subdued lights so long as the baby was all right. *Please* let him be all right!

The desperation in her eyes made Liam bite back his instinctive response that he wasn't in a position to know what she'd planned, he had been excluded. 'You're a spontaneous sort of lady—our baby obviously takes after you.'

Our baby. The words brought weak tears to her eyes. One little word and suddenly the burden of worry and responsibility was shared.

'Are you in pain?' he asked sharply.

'No.' She reached out to stop him pressing the emergency buzzer. 'I just feel pretty tired. Actually I can hardly keep my eyes open.'

'Why bother?' he said softly. He adjusted the overhead light so the glare didn't shine in her eyes.

Jo took his point. 'It will be all right, won't it?' she asked sleepily. Even though she knew he wasn't in a position to guarantee anything, the warm confidence in his smile eased her fears.

'Definitely. Just go to sleep while you can.'

As it happened that wasn't very long. Jo was awoken several hours later by the pain. 'Something's happening.'

When Liam's fingers tightened around hers she realised she'd fallen asleep holding his hand. 'Shall I get someone?' Liam's body, greyhound lean, was almost quivering under the rush of adrenaline that surged through his body.

Despite the ungainly bulk of her body, her physical frailty had never been more apparent. It made him feel physically sick to know what sort of ordeal she was going to go through and he was helpless to prevent it. He couldn't understand why reasonably sane people did this sort of thing more than once!

Jo was fully awake now. 'I think you better had.' She felt suddenly calm and this new serenity was reflected in her voice.

There wasn't much time to worry; things moved too fast from that moment onwards. Liam had been right—all the worry and pain became a memory the instant the midwife laid the warm body of her baby on her chest. She'd never forget the warmth and softness of the tiny body she traced with trembling hands. The wondrous moment was all too brief; they wrapped him in a foil blanket and whisked him away.

'He's fine,' the midwife said in reply to her anxious enquiry, 'just a little small. We want to keep him warm.'

Inexplicably Liam was reluctant to go. Jo was baffled and frustrated by his attitude. 'Please, one of us should be with him. I can't bear the idea of him being alone.' Her voice was sharp with anxiety. For a man who had gone to extraordinary lengths to be a part of his son's life, he'd shown only fleeting interest in him since he'd put in his appearance.

A possible explanation for his attitude presented itself. 'Are you disappointed? Did you want a girl?' Things like that mattered to some people, or so she'd heard.

'Disappointed?' Liam collapsed onto the chair beside her bed and gave a strange laugh. 'You've had too much of this stuff.' He flicked the mask which had supplied a miraculous mixture of gas and air during the height of her contractions. 'I'm...' He rolled his eyes heavenwards whilst searching appropriate words to describe how he felt. 'Elated doesn't do this feeling justice,' he admitted huskily.

Their eyes locked in a moment of complete understanding. 'I know what you mean.' Her throat ached with emotion as she stored away this precious golden moment of complete harmony.

'You're crying, Jo.' He blotted a stray tear from her cheek with the tip of his finger.

'If like every other male on the planet you hadn't been practising not to since you were five years old I expect you would be too.' She sniffed. The expression in his eyes had told her that he was as emotionally overwhelmed by the birth of their child as she was. 'Will you go and see him and tell me how he is...*pleeease*, Liam?'

'Don't worry, we'll look after her for you,' the midwife informed him kindly when he still displayed some reluctance to leave her. 'I don't think he trusts us, dear,' she added with a smile in Jo's direction.

Liam didn't dispute this claim. 'You can't get rid of me so easily. I'll be back!'

'I'm sure he will,' the midwife murmured with an unprofessional sigh. 'Some girls have all the luck!' she observed with a tinge of envy. 'It's lovely to see a couple who are so close.'

Who am I to dispel her romantic fantasy? Jo thought, smiling weakly. In her overtired brain Liam's straightforward words had taken on a sinister significance: he was staking a claim—a claim that, thanks to her gullibility, he could back up legally. Giving birth was going to look easy once they sat down and sorted out the details of their future.

'It really feels like he's mine now we're home.'

'*Mine?*'

Jo caught her upper lip between her teeth but didn't reply to his ironic interjection. 'When I was visiting him every day in hospital it felt as if he belonged to someone else.' Every container in the room appeared to be filled with floral tributes; the smell was marvellous. 'People have been kind,' she murmured, reading a label attached to a bouquet.

The awkwardness with which she stood uncertainly looking around the room was not wasted on Liam. She'd said 'home' but the fact she didn't feel she belonged had never been more obvious.

'It'll certainly be easier to say goodnight to him in the nursery rather than travelling twenty miles to the hospital,' he agreed casually. 'Here, let me hold him for you,' he said as she began to shrug her jacket off one shoulder. 'Don't worry, I'm not about to flee the country,' he added with a flicker of anger in his eyes as she very obviously hesitated, only fractionally, but enough to betray her reluctance to relinquish her burden.

'We've discussed this often enough, Jo. I thought the

whole idea of you being here is for me to help you until you have some sort of routine.'

'I thought the idea was you're going to be indispensable.'

She handed over the travel seat containing the sleeping figure of their son regretting her churlish response, but unable to admit it. Whilst she'd been longing for this moment for the past weeks she'd also been dreading it. How were you supposed to act when circumstances beyond your control meant you were forced to share a house with your estranged husband?

To say she had doubts over this arrangement would have been an understatement! But when she'd looked at it from a dispassionate point of view—which Liam had forced her to—this was the best solution to her immediate problems.

There had been Dad, but she knew her father had been secretly relieved when she'd said she was moving in with Liam when little Connor came out of hospital. She didn't blame him—Dad's days of being kept awake by crying babies were behind him.

Looking after a baby when there were professionals around to step in was one thing, but being alone with sole responsibility for that life…! Connor had had a few setbacks over the past three weeks. If anything happened now there was no medical team to spring into action. Was she being pathetic not going solo from the start?

So long as I remember this was only a temporary solution I can cope with the arrangement, she told herself firmly. She'd been over all the arguments in her head often enough.

'You think I'll try and persuade you to stay when the time comes? Don't you?' Liam removed the blanket that covered the sleeping baby; the room was warm.

His words made Jo start, almost guiltily. 'Your mother

didn't believe a word I said when I told her this was strictly temporary.' She shook her head wearily. 'And my dad wasn't much better.'

'I'm not talking about what other people think, I'm talking about what you think. The fact you feel the need to qualify every other sentence you utter with a veiled reference to the fact you'll only be here for a few weeks makes it pretty clear you think I'm going to develop selective amnesia.'

She flushed and turned away from his ironic stare. Surely she'd been more subtle than that? 'You'll probably be so desperate for a decent night's sleep you'll call us a taxi.'

She didn't feel half as flippant as she sounded but she was determined not to let things get too intense and confusing. She couldn't let herself be influenced by her own feelings for him. Liam only wanted her because she came as a package with the baby. She couldn't settle for that, could she? In her weaker moments she found herself thinking perhaps it wouldn't be so bad after all. No, if she started making concessions she was lost!

'You're wrong, you know.'

'You'll make us walk...?' Her nervous humour was met by a very unappreciative audience. Would she want to walk? That was the question. When it came to the crunch would she have the strength?

'I don't want you to stay, Jo—not if you don't trust me.'

It was a lot like the feeling she'd experienced on her first real date—at least she'd thought at the time it was a real date, when she'd stood heart pounding in anticipation, ready to be kissed, and the boy in question had gruffly confided that he fancied her best friend to distraction. Take that feeling and multiply it by a million or so and you were almost there. *Liam didn't want her.* That sort of simplified matters, but did she really want things that simple?

'Let me get this straight—you don't want me to live with you?' She was surprised that her voice sounded almost normal.

'You're welcome to stay as long as you need to,' he said, not exactly falling over himself to contradict her.

'Very grateful, I'm sure.' It was all a matter of self-control. This was the wrong time to hyperventilate—having Liam shove her face in a brown paper bag would really be the icing on the cake!

Did he feel this terrible when I rejected him? She discarded this theory; nobody had *ever* felt this bad. 'But you're attaching…conditions to me extending my stay. Have I got it right?' Her voice shook with suppressed emotions, one of which was definitely anger. She concentrated on anger; it was a much easier emotion than devastation or humiliation. *How dare he say he doesn't want me, even if it's true?*

'I expect you'll feel happier knowing I'm not going to pressurise you. Sit down, you look washed out.' Apparently oblivious to the fact his words had brought her to the brink of an emotional explosion, he placed the baby carrier down and plumped up a cushion on the armchair. 'It's bound to be a bit of an anticlimax. You've been building up to this day for so long now.'

Very understanding for an insensitive rat, she marvelled. 'You will tell me when I've outstayed my welcome, won't you?'

'Have I said something to upset you?'

Now she was *sure* he was being sarcastic. 'You think I'd be that impossible to live with, then?' It would have been more dignified to hold her tongue—dignified, but impossible. 'Or are you just afraid I'll disrupt your social life?'

'I think your distrust of me would be a major obstacle,' he informed her calmly. 'For different reasons I've simply come to the same conclusion as you. Don't you find it just the tiniest bit perverse that you're offended?'

'I am not offended.' She wished she'd held her tongue and hadn't given him the opportunity to gloat. Too late to worry about that now.

One dark, sceptical brow disappeared behind the dark hank of hair that had flopped forward over his forehead. 'Perhaps you've been enjoying the spectacle of me begging and cajoling you,' he mused. 'It must have given you a delicious sense of power.' His voice was controlled but his reflective smile was caustic. 'Now when I make it clear there is no way I'm going to try slipping into your bed and seducing you...' With narrowed eyes he repeated the comments Jo recalled making during their lengthy, and sometimes heated debates in hospital. 'I must say you have a lamentably low opinion of my will-power.'

Why doesn't he just go ahead and say he doesn't find me attractive any more? She certainly didn't feel very attractive at the moment. Motherhood had made her many things, but irresistibly sexy was not one of them. She'd always known the sexual thing had been a temporary, crazy thing that would die a natural death. There was no need at all to be devastated just because he chose to spell it out.

'The last time your will-power was put to the test I don't recall you emerging with flying colours!' Liam's expression didn't alter, but that muscle with a life of its own in his left cheek started pulsing spasmodically. So, it was below the belt. She refused to feel repentant; he'd pushed her into a corner.

Power? The man was mad. Power was the last thing she'd had. She'd been as helpless as a newborn babe since she'd realised she'd fallen in love with him.

'And from where I was sitting it looked more like bullying and blackmailing than cajoling!' Who was he kidding? He'd never begged in his life.

He ignored her heated words with an infuriatingly sceptical smile. 'I've had enough of trying to fit in with your plans. If you want to stay it'll be on my terms.'

'How masterful!' she hooted derisively.

'It's the new me. Glad you like it.'

'I don't!'

'If you want me, Jo, you'll have to do the asking.'

She gasped incredulously. 'What a time to start experimenting with mind-altering substances,' she croaked.

'I'd be willing to think again. Probably...'

'For the sake of the baby, no doubt.'

'I'm not sure if having two parents sharing a roof is enough compensation for bringing a child up in an atmosphere of mistrust.'

'And your version of trust means I have to believe everything you tell me no matter how implausible.'

'Why would I lie to you?' He pushed back the errant wing of hair impatiently. The simplicity of his question troubled her.

'You need a haircut,' she observed automatically.

He gritted his teeth. For a second there it had looked as if she had actually paused long enough to think. 'That's a very wifely observation,' he hissed. 'It brings to mind all the wifely things I've been missing.'

This acid retort brought a flush to her cheeks. 'If I've got to look at you, you might at least be presentable.' She also had enough to contend with without fighting her irrational urges to brush that lock of hair from his eyes.

'What is this, snipe as you mean to go on?'

'I am not…' Under his steady regard she had the grace to blush.

She was suddenly assailed by guilt. He'd been so good to her during the last worrying weeks. Whenever she'd needed him he'd been there and all he'd got for his troubles was an ungrateful female who took out her fears and frustrations on him. No wonder he wanted to see the back of her.

'It's your fault!' she yelled unreasonably.

'I've grown to expect something more inspired from you, Jo,' he said in a disappointed tone.

The unmistakable snuffling sounds of Connor waking diverted her frustration. Her body was programmed to respond to the hungry cry. 'He'll want feeding.' She'd heard that some men resented the fact their partners had to drop everything for a new baby; Liam wasn't displaying any of this resentment.

'I'll get you a drink and shift your gear to the nursery,' he said practically as she settled down with the baby on her lap.

The implication of her things being put in the nursery didn't escape her. A short time later when she took Connor through to his crib the sight of the single bed against one wall made it pretty clear Liam wasn't risking any misunderstandings.

'I didn't think you'd want to be far from him.'

Jo twisted around; she hadn't heard his silent approach. 'That's very thoughtful.'

'Thoughtful to let you have the sleepless nights?'

She shrugged. 'You can't feed him.'

'No, but I can hear him and bring him to you when he needs a feed. We'll take turns sleeping in here until you feel more comfortable leaving him alone.' Unexpectedly he took her chin in his fingers and tilted her face upwards. 'He only stopped breathing that time because of the infection,' he said compassionately. 'You heard what the doctors said, he's strong.' Liam looked at the small, sleeping figure with affectionate pride.

Her heart swelled with love. Without his support she didn't think she could have survived the last few weeks of constant worry and uncertainty. At one point it had seemed that Connor was taking two steps backwards for every one forward but Liam's confidence had not wavered for an instant.

'I'm glad I'm not alone.' She couldn't regret the spontaneity of her fierce little announcement, but she couldn't help but wonder, given their recent exchange of views, how he'd take it.

Liam's gaze shifted abruptly to her face. Her words had obviously shocked him. 'You'll never be alone now, Jo.'

She couldn't tear her gaze away from his staggeringly beautiful eyes. 'No?' she breathed huskily.

'No, you have Connor.'

She might be in love with their son—he was the most perfect creature ever born—but that hadn't been what she'd hoped to hear. She turned her head away and hoped he didn't suspect how close she'd come to making a complete fool of herself.

'For the next eighteen years, anyway.' She had control of her feelings by the time she replied.

'All his mates will fancy you like crazy,' Liam predicted.

'Teenagers think sex is a distant memory to anyone over thirty.'

'No, that's just their parents. Boys of that age always find the experienced older woman irresistible.'

'Could this be the wisdom of experience talking?' Jo

lifted her face to him, a teasing smile on her lips. Sparring with Liam had always been an enjoyable way to pass the time.

'Quite like old times.'

He'd done it so often she didn't feel surprised that Liam's words mirrored her thoughts almost exactly.

'It's not, though, is it?' She spoilt the moment by stating the obvious.

'That doesn't have to be a bad thing—it's up to us.' He cursed as the phone he carried shrilly rang out. 'I thought I'd turned it off, sorry. Excuse me a sec.' He fished out his mobile and shot an anxious look at the sleeping baby before speaking tersely into the receiver. 'Suzanna, I told you I'm not available today. Two minutes, that's all...' He mimed 'sorry' at Jo and stepped out of the room.

Well, the woman must be moonstruck if she didn't mind being spoken to like that, Jo reflected. It had hardly been lover-like. Had she minded him taking such an active part in the first few weeks of his son's life? Obviously other parts of their relationship compensated... Perhaps they had great sex? There were distinct disadvantages to having a vivid imagination! She closed her eyes and willed the Technicolor images to recede.

'Sorry about that.'

Jo stepped outside the room past Liam who pushed the door quietly to behind her. The jealousy tightened like a knot in her chest until she felt as if she couldn't breathe.

'You don't have to apologise for your personal life to me. It's not as if we're really married.' She oozed mature understanding.

'Just like you're not really jealous.'

The mature understanding vanished into thin air. 'If you spoke to me like that, I'd...I'd...'

'How fortunate for humanity all that wild red-headed aggression is confined in a delicate and fragile vessel.'

Lucky for him too, she thought as her hands automatically balled into fists. 'She must be *besotted*!' Jo spat, eyeing him with venomous dislike.

'Do you think so?'

'You're asking *me* for reassurance? I didn't think you were plagued by insecurities.'

'I used to think that too—possibly marrying a woman who runs out on me on our wedding night has sapped my confidence.'

'It doesn't show.'

He laid a hand on her arm and she felt the fine quiver of tension run through his body. Confused, she raised her eyes to his face. The intensity of the pain she glimpsed in his shadowed eyes was shocking. Suddenly she wasn't certain about anything any more.

'I didn't want to hurt you,' she whispered. 'I was partly to blame. I allowed myself to have some pretty unrealistic expectations of our marriage,' she confessed, 'and when I heard you...' She closed her eyes as she relived the awful moment. 'I realised how stupid I'd been,' she finished flatly.

Liam moved until she stood within the circle of his arms. His thumbs moved in circular, rhythmic motions over her upper arms. Her eyelids fluttered but she couldn't look away from the devouring grip of his gaze.

'How had you been stupid, Jo?' His voice sounded raw and uneven, but the way his tongue curled around her name triggered a terrifying response in her body. 'You're hot,' he breathed wonderingly as a pink glow suffused her from head to toe. 'Did I...?'

She was suddenly tired: tired of pretending, tired of denying the obvious. 'I can't help it.' She raked her quivering lower lip quite savagely with her teeth. 'I thought I could do this,' she moaned half to herself. Her silky hair lashed against her cheek as she shook her head from side to side. 'But obviously I can't.'

He reached down and brushed away a strand that had adhered to the film of moisture that covered her skin. 'Tell me about your unrealistic dreams, Jo.'

'I thought I could make you fall in love with me.' She hunched her shoulders defensively.

'That's not something you can engineer, it just happens. Did it happen to you, Jo?'

His pursuit of the truth seemed unreasonably cruel but part of her was relieved to be able to finally confess. 'Yes...yes...yes!' She tried to cover her face with her hands, but cruelly he took her wrists.

'No,' he said firmly as she struggled, 'I think you've hidden from me for long enough. Look at me!' he ordered quietly.

Something she couldn't quite identify in his tone made her obey without thinking. One large tear trembled in the corner of her eyes before it slowly slid down the curve of her cheek as she stood transfixed by what she was seeing. All thoughts of escape disappeared. Caution had become a habit and she found she couldn't accept what she was seeing.

'Shall *I* confess something?' There was an expression in his eyes she'd only ever seen in her dreams, and it was better—*so much* better in real life.

Jo nodded her head vigorously. She had a sudden blissful feeling she might quite like what she was about to hear.

'If you'd stayed at that door a few moments longer you'd have heard me tell Dad the only reason I'd married you was that I loved you. I loved you and I couldn't bear the idea of living without you. I thought that was what you'd heard. I thought that was what made you so disgusted. Would you believe I was relieved when I realised you'd got the wrong end of the stick—as usual?'

'You love me?' she echoed stupidly. All that pain and anguish and he'd loved her all along. It wouldn't sink in. 'Why didn't you tell me?' she cried.

'If you let your mind wander back you might realise that I was trying to! You didn't make it easy. It's very awkward to discover you want to tear the clothes off the back of someone you've treated like...'

'One of the lads...?'

'Your sex has never been in dispute. Your taste in men, now that's another matter.'

'Yes...well.' The bubble of confidence inside was expanding until she was floating on a cloud of euphoria. 'I was a bit jealous myself.'

'I made up the Suzanna, in the letters.'

'She looked pretty real to me!' She closed her eyes and rubbed her cheek lovingly against his arm. I'm not dreaming, she told herself. This is real. A wondering smile curved her generous lips as she opened her eyes.

'Oh, I borrowed the name without even realising it because the real Suzanna was getting in my hair at the time, being a damned nuisance as it happened. God, that woman's persistent! She'd put together a financial package and she was convinced it would all fall apart if I didn't stop dragging my feet. I wasn't being deliberately hard to get, I just wasn't prepared to commit myself to anything I hadn't thoroughly researched.

'The idea of me getting married before I'd finished polishing up the script nearly gave her an apoplexy. I shouldn't be ungrateful—they're paying me an indecent amount of money and I've already been offered an advance on my next book.'

So long as Suzanna only wanted his literary talent Jo could feel quite benevolent about her. 'Why would you do a thing like make up a woman?' Amazingly she found she could smile at his stupidity. Liam loved her, she could smile at just about anything! 'Were you trying to make me jealous?' she asked, indignant at this sudden possibility.

'I might have tried it if I'd thought it would work, but my motivation was much less complex. I went away with every intention of forgetting our night of unbridled passion—as instructed. Sensible plan, only I couldn't seem to get my head around it. I was as anxious as you were to preserve our friendship and I was sure if you suspected I couldn't stop thinking about...' His eyes were hot and sultry as they sought hers. 'Do you know you give this little cry—real deep and husky when...?'

He took the fingers she'd hurriedly placed over his lips into his mouth and slowly ran his tongue over each one, watching her eyes darken and glaze as he did so. 'Yeah, that's the one,' he agreed huskily. 'Just thinking about it makes the hair on my neck stand on end.'

'What else does it do to you, Liam?'

'I'll show you very shortly,' he promised huskily. 'I created Suzanna to stop you suspecting I was getting a mild case of obsession.'

'Only mild?' Her lips pursed provocatively in mock dissatisfaction.

'You want your pound of flesh? Fine. I'm talking sleep deprivation, loss of appetite and the attention span of a flea. Satisfied?'

'Do fleas have a problem with concentration, then?' From the instant he'd mentioned flesh—specifically his— her brain had been reminding her of exactly how perfect the texture of Liam's was.

'How the hell should I know?' he exclaimed indignantly.

'Do you know the skin on your back feels quite different from your stomach?' Her heavy, slumbrously sexy gaze ran down his body. When she moistened her dry lips with the tip of her tongue and sighed Liam let out a low moan. 'What's wrong?' she asked anxiously. 'Are you in pain?'

'Definitely!'

'Is there anything I can do to help?'

'I can bring several things to mind offhand,' he admitted throatily.

'Is this one of them?' On tiptoe she reached up and took his face between her hands. Her parted lips trembled against his and as his tongue thrust deep into the velvety darkness of her mouth her bones liquefied. 'I've missed the taste of you—you can have no idea, Liam! I've dreamt of your kiss, my love.'

He tasted warm and spicy, and she breathed in the fragrance of his warm body greedily. His teeth closed over the fullness of her lower lip and he tugged before allowing his tongue to trace the inner full curve of her sweet mouth. Her hands slid open-palmed down his chest and a low series of noisy gasps emerged from her parted lips.

He took her face almost roughly between his hands and examined her delicate features hungrily.

'I can't imagine why I didn't realise how shamefully beautiful you are years ago.'

'I'm not beautiful, Liam. My mouth is too big, my—'

'I want to get something straight right now,' he said, placing a finger to her lips. 'Have you forgotten what I said? You're only allowed to stay if you accept my terms and the first one of those is when I tell you you're beautiful and desirable there will be no arguments.'

'Whatever you say, Liam,' she said meekly.

'I could throttle you when I think of the past few months.'

'That might be counter-productive,' she suggested gently as she wove her fingers deeper into his hair.

'You've got a point there,' he agreed, as the top button on her blouse popped open.

'When did you realise you loved me?'

Liam removed his gaze from the shadowy promise of her cleavage reluctantly. 'Now isn't that just like a woman, as my old dad would say?'

'Are you avoiding the question?'

'I'm warning you this isn't your standard romantic reply. It wasn't when the sunlight turned your hair into a burnished halo or anything like that.'

She got hold of his shirt and pretended to shake him. 'I want to know.'

'It was when you'd been so sick that evening at your place. I walked in and you were sitting there on the floor and you looked up at me. You looked like death,' he recalled with inappropriate accuracy, but Jo forgave him because the wonder he'd felt then was still fresh in his eyes for her to see now. 'Your eyes seemed to fill half your face and there were black circles under them. Your skin was so white I could have counted your freckles.' A slow smile curved his lips and he shook his head incredulously. 'I just looked at you and thought, I want to look at that face every day of my life. I felt incredibly stupid that I'd not realised it before.'

'Who told you you're not romantic?' She sniffed.

'You.'

'I think I'm going to cry.'

'Kiss me instead.'

Being an obedient wife, Jo did just that.

'Is he asleep?' Liam whispered.

'I think so.' Jo strained to see the features of their young son in the pale dawn light. He lay between them in the king-size bed.

'Shall I put him back in the crib?'

Jo flicked on the bedside light. 'Yes, he's sound asleep.' She smiled, looking at the face of cherubic innocence. 'He's a miracle, isn't he?'

'A miracle with excellent lungs, I'm happy to say.' Liam carefully placed the sleeping infant in the crib at the foot of the bed.

Jo watched him covetously. Her husband slept naked and the sight of his beautiful, streamlined body made her unconsciously lick her lips.

'I think I prefer the simplified sleeping arrangements,' he said.

'You might not be so enthusiastic after a few more sleepless nights.'

Liam slid back into the bed beside her and placed his rangy frame up against her. 'A man on his honeymoon doesn't expect to sleep.'

'Is that where we are?'

'I don't know about you, love, but I'm in heaven.' He reached out for her and gathered her pliable, warm body to him. 'You'll get overheated with this on.'

'You're probably right,' she murmured as the nightshirt was tossed across the room.

'I missed so much.' His head rested against her shoulder and his hand was spread out over her belly.

The deep regret and loss in his voice brought a lump to her throat. 'I wanted to share it too, Liam. I wanted you to feel our baby move.'

'Our baby is here and so are you; that's all that matters to me, Jo.' His hand moved slowly down her quivering body from shoulder to flank. 'You've forgotten something, though.'

'I have?' she said thickly, allowing her tongue to trace a damp trail over his shoulder. She'd forgotten about feeling unattractive. Liam made her feel the most desirable woman on earth.

'I said you'd have to do the asking.'

'And if I don't?'

'I'll have to be inconsistent and make love to you anyway.'

'In that case,' she said smugly as she insinuated a leg between his thighs and applied a gentle amount of pressure, 'will you please allow me to stay with you, Liam, and share my body with you? My heart I throw in for free,' she offered generously. She yelped as he flipped her over onto her back without warning.

'Is that an unconditional offer?' he growled

She smiled with sultry sincerity into his eyes. 'You'd better believe it, my love.'

Liam did.

EXPECTING

She's sexy, she's successful... and she's pregnant!

Relax and enjoy these new stories about spirited women and gorgeous men, whose passion results in pregnancies... sometimes unexpectedly! All the new parents-to-be will discover that the business of making babies brings with it the most special love of all....

Harlequin Presents® brings you one **EXPECTING!** book each month throughout 1999.

Look out for:

The Unexpected Father by Kathryn Ross
Harlequin Presents® #2022, April 1999

The Playboy's Baby by Mary Lyons
Harlequin Presents® #2028, May 1999

Accidental Baby by Kim Lawrence
Harlequin Presents® #2034, June 1999

The Unexpected Baby by Diana Hamilton
Harlequin Presents® #2040, July 1999

Available wherever Harlequin books are sold.

HARLEQUIN®
Makes any time special ™

If you enjoyed what you just read,
then we've got an offer you can't resist!

Take 2 bestselling love stories FREE!

Plus get a FREE surprise gift!

Clip this page and mail it to Harlequin Reader Service®

IN U.S.A.
3010 Walden Ave.
P.O. Box 1867
Buffalo, N.Y. 14240-1867

IN CANADA
P.O. Box 609
Fort Erie, Ontario
L2A 5X3

YES! Please send me 2 free Harlequin Presents® novels and my free surprise gift. Then send me 6 brand-new novels every month, which I will receive months before they're available in stores. In the U.S.A., bill me at the bargain price of $3.12 plus 25¢ delivery per book and applicable sales tax, if any*. In Canada, bill me at the bargain price of $3.49 plus 25¢ delivery per book and applicable taxes**. That's the complete price and a savings of over 10% off the cover prices—what a great deal! I understand that accepting the 2 free books and gift places me under no obligation ever to buy any books. I can always return a shipment and cancel at any time. Even if I never buy another book from Harlequin, the 2 free books and gift are mine to keep forever. So why not take us up on our invitation. You'll be glad you did!

106 HEN CNER
306 HEN CNES

Name	(PLEASE PRINT)	
Address	Apt.#	
City	State/Prov.	Zip/Postal Code

* Terms and prices subject to change without notice. Sales tax applicable in N.Y.
** Canadian residents will be charged applicable provincial taxes and GST.
All orders subject to approval. Offer limited to one per household.
® are registered trademarks of Harlequin Enterprises Limited.

PRES99   ©1998 Harlequin Enterprises Limited

HARLEQUIN ◆ PRESENTS®

THE BARONS

One sister, three brothers— who will inherit, and will they all find lovers?

Jonas is approaching his eighty-fifth birthday, and he's decided it's time to choose the heir of his sprawling ranch, Espada. He has three ruggedly good-looking sons, Gage, Travis and Slade, and a beautiful stepdaughter, Caitlin.

Who will receive Baron's bequest? As the Baron brothers and their sister discover, there's more at stake than Espada. For love also has its part to play in deciding their futures....

Enjoy Gage's story:
Marriage on the Edge
Harlequin Presents #2027, May 1999

And in August, get to know Travis a whole lot better in
More than a Mistress
Harlequin Presents #2045

Available wherever Harlequin books are sold.

◆ HARLEQUIN®
Makes any time special ™

HARLEQUIN ✦ PRESENTS®

Wedded Bliss

Penny Jordan   Carole Mortimer

Two brand-new stories—for the price of one!—
in one easy-to-read volume.
Especially written by your favorite authors!

Wedded Bliss
Harlequin Presents #2031, June 1999
THEY'RE WED AGAIN!
by Penny Jordan
and
THE MAN SHE'LL MARRY
by Carole Mortimer

There's nothing more exciting than a wedding!
Share the excitement as two couples make their very
different journeys which will take them up the aisle to
embark upon a life of happiness!

Available **next month** wherever Harlequin books
are sold.

✦ HARLEQUIN®
Makes any time special™

Look us up on-line at: http://www.romance.net   HP2IN1

Coming Next Month

HARLEQUIN PRESENTS®

THE BEST HAS JUST GOTTEN BETTER!

#2037 THE SPANISH GROOM Lynne Graham
To please his ailing godfather, Cesar Valverde agreed to marry
Dixie Robinson. Unexpectedly, he found her to be an achingly
sensual woman. So within a week, his fake fiancée had
become his wife and become pregnant!

#2038 THE SECRET MISTRESS Emma Darcy
Presents Passion
Luis Martinez had never forgiven Shontelle for walking away
from their affair. But now she needed his help, and Luis saw a
way to exact vengeance for his wounded pride: he'd keep her
safe in exchange for one night in her bed...

#2039 TO WOO A WIFE Carole Mortimer
Bachelor Brothers
As a beautiful, young widow, Abbie was wary of emotional
and physical involvement. Jarrett was used to being a winner
in the boardroom and the bedroom, so to him, Abbie was the
ultimate challenge: she needed wooing!

#2040 HE'S MY HUSBAND! Lindsay Armstrong
Nicola was Brett's wife of convenience, but it seemed to
her that he had other admirers. Nicola loved Brett and his
children, so the time had come to show everyone, including
Brett, exactly whose husband he really was!

#2041 THE UNEXPECTED BABY Diana Hamilton
Expecting!
Elena was deeply in love with her brand-new husband, Jed, so
discovering she was pregnant should have completed her joy.
Elena knew she'd have to tell Jed, but would their marriage
survive the truth?

#2042 REMARRIED IN HASTE Sandra Field
Brant Curtis had dreamed about his ex-wife, Rowan, for years,
and now he was face-to-face with her. He didn't have a plan,
but he wanted more than a one night stand for old times'
sake—he wanted his wife back, whatever it took!